LUST EVER AFTER

ROSE DE FER

mischief

This novel is entirely a work of fiction.
The names, characters and incidents portrayed in it are
the work of the author's imagination. Any resemblance to
actual persons, living or dead, events or localities is
entirely coincidental.

Mischief
An imprint of HarperCollins*Publishers*
77–85 Fulham Palace Road,
Hammersmith, London W6 8JB

www.mischiefbooks.com

A Paperback Original 2013

First published in Great Britain in ebook format by
HarperCollins*Publishers* 2012

Copyright © Rose de Fer 2013

Rose de Fer asserts the moral right to
be identified as the author of this work

A catalogue record for this book is
available from the British Library

ISBN-13: 9780007553143

CONTENTS

CHAPTER ONE

The Anatomy Lesson

'And so, gentlemen, although this is a purely scientific demonstration, you can see that the subject is nonetheless displaying clear and unequivocal signs of arousal.'

The girl, Daisy, was indeed very flushed. She lay naked and splayed on the rugged wooden table in the centre of the room, her skin glowing in the light from the paraffin lamps. Some two dozen young men in frock coats and cravats peered down into the arena of the small operating theatre. Daisy heard the creak of floorboards and the rustle of fabric as they shifted to get a better view. Although she was quite warm, gooseflesh rose on her skin as Dr Frankenstein trailed his fingers over her body, pointing out various features of her anatomy. She was finding it very difficult to remain still, despite his frequent admonishments.

'This specimen is particularly responsive,' Frankenstein

said, his voice crisp and cultured, his hands adept and precise. 'Observe how her nipples react to even the slightest stimulation.'

Daisy felt them respond just as he described, stiffening instantly. His fingertips gently touched the hard little peaks and she gasped, throwing her head back and pressing her thighs together around the hot pulse she felt quickening there. She trembled, fingering the leather restraints on either side of the table.

As though reading her mind, the doctor said, 'If you can't be still, my girl, I will have to use those.'

Her eyes closed and she blushed deeply, struggling to obey. She was unaccustomed to the sensation of being fully naked, let alone so exposed before an audience. A group of gentlemen at that. It created a heady mix of feelings within her: guilt, titillation, fear, excitement.

She reminded herself of what the doctor had told her when he had recruited her for this demonstration. She would be helping her fellow man, assisting in the advancement of medical science and the understanding of human anatomy. There was nothing untoward about his proposal, nothing for her to feel ashamed about. On the contrary, she should be proud of the service she would be providing. And he would give her a gold sovereign for her trouble. She couldn't hope to make that in a week selling books in her father's shop.

'It is of vital importance,' he had told her, 'that students of medicine should have a complete understanding of the form and physiology of the fairer sex. Should they really be expected to make guesses based on vague sketches or genteel allusions to "down there" by embarrassed female patients?'

'I'll do my best,' she had told him at last, both frightened and exhilarated by her decision. 'Er ... there's no need to inform my father, is there?'

Another jolt of nearly unbearable pleasure brought her back to the moment and she gripped the restraints tightly, secretly wishing she were bound. That way she could pretend that this was all against her will. In fact, the idea made her even more lightheaded with desire.

'Very sensitive indeed,' Frankenstein was saying. Now he was pinching her tender nipples, rolling them softly between finger and thumb.

Daisy panted and writhed on the table, her body arching lewdly. She couldn't help its wanton responses, nor the positively obscene thoughts she found accompanying them. She imagined the students crowding round to examine her themselves in even more intimate detail. A dozen pairs of hands stroking her thighs, her breasts, her bottom. Curious fingers exploring and invading every orifice. Strong arms holding her down if she struggled too much.

'Hysteria is a pervasive underlying condition, gentlemen, present only in the female of the species.

It disorders the mind and frustrates the body. You can see for yourselves how easily it is manifested, even in such impersonal surroundings as these. I believe that all women suffer from it to some degree. Fortunately, with the technological advancements of our modern age, it is quite treatable.' He paused to smile up at his audience. 'Not to mention extremely lucrative.'

The room hummed with polite laughter and a few murmurs of admiration. Daisy didn't fully understand what they were talking about. Naturally, she had heard the term 'hysteria' before. She had once seen a lady swoon in her father's shop, having caught sight of the volumes he kept behind his desk for private subscribers. It hadn't occurred to her at the time that the lady was in a state comparable to the one she found herself in now. But she had peeked at those volumes later herself and the doctor was right; the experience had left her feeling quite inflamed.

'A lady clearly cannot function in such a state,' Frankenstein continued, 'and the mental turbulence must be released by physical means.'

'And this device you spoke of can actually cure it?' came a voice from somewhere above her.

'Alas, no,' Frankenstein said. 'The affliction is incurable. But with regular treatments one may at least provide temporary relief. As my thriving practice can attest.'

He went on to describe a steam-powered device called

the Alleviator, which produced intense vibrations and very quickly achieved the curative 'paroxysm' that physicians found so tedious and difficult to administer by hand. As he explained the process, he gently prised Daisy's legs apart and placed his hand against her sex, making her whimper with longing. She was extremely wet, an observation Frankenstein immediately shared with the watchers. It only made her wetter. If she hadn't been hysterical before, she most certainly was now.

She couldn't help recalling some of the pictures she had seen in one of those forbidden volumes – strange Oriental drawings of men and women unclothed, in astonishing positions, performing acts she wouldn't have imagined possible. The pictures had made her blush and tingle and her sex had throbbed much as it was doing now. She felt herself drowning in the sensation as he described the procedure in more detail and answered several questions about the mechanics of the device.

The situation was dizzyingly erotic for Daisy. The doctor never once called her by name; he merely referred to her as 'the subject'. And yet somehow his impersonal manner only enhanced her arousal. Her entire body felt inflamed, all her senses heightened. Frankenstein urged her legs wider apart and with his fingers he spread her open. She closed her eyes, awash with the sense of exposure and the peculiar pleasure it brought her.

She wasn't sure she wanted to experience this

'paroxysm' if it would *relieve* her symptoms of hysteria. The physical hunger was itself wildly pleasurable and she didn't want it to end. Indeed, every time he touched her, however dispassionately, she felt her heart race faster.

One of the students spoke up. 'Sir, may we ask for a demonstration of how this device works?'

'Ah, no,' Frankenstein said. 'Unfortunately, the device is too large to transport. I keep it in a special private chamber in my consulting rooms. The ladies must come to me, you see.'

Daisy tried to imagine the apparatus and found she grew even more excited by the picture her mind was creating. She saw herself standing before a huge contraption of cold steel, twisting her hands nervously as she waited to surrender her body to its treatment. At Dr Frankenstein's instruction, she removed her dress and wore only her chemise. A hooded assistant, with smooth feminine hands, helped her up onto a wide wooden platform. She eased Daisy onto her back on a gleaming metal table and fastened her arms tightly above her head with manacles. Then she pulled Daisy's legs wide apart, securing them with iron bands around her knees and ankles. The position left her sex completely exposed.

Daisy heard a deep rumbling as the steam engine roared to life and the entire structure began to throb around her. There was the low hum of voices as Dr Frankenstein and his lady assistant discussed various settings for the machine and moved around Daisy making adjustments. She heard the sound of a crank turning, the clank and rattle of a chain, and she looked up to see a strange mechanism being lowered into position between her legs. It too was made of cold steel and shaped like the male parts she had seen in the forbidden books. Unable to escape, she had no choice but to submit as Dr Frankenstein pushed the mechanism deep inside her, making her cry out. The assistant told her softly to be quiet and she bit back a cry as the device began to pump like a piston, in and out, in and out. She strained against her bonds to reassure herself that she was held fast.

She closed her eyes as a pair of soft hands untied the laces of her chemise, exposing her full breasts. Helpless and fully on display, Daisy surrendered to the exquisite sensations as the assistant caressed her. The cold machine ravished her while warm human hands cupped her breasts, tweaking the nipples. As had been pointed out to the roomful of students, she was highly responsive. The enormous engine bombarded her with pleasure so intense she wasn't sure she could take it. Then the lady lowered her head to Daisy's breasts, pressing her lips against –

'But, sir, surely you don't intend to leave the girl in such a state?'

The voice startled Daisy from her fantasy and she opened her eyes, surprised for a moment to find herself back in the operating theatre and not strapped into the steel contraption.

'Certainly not,' Frankenstein said, 'but, given the state of extreme arousal in the subject, I don't imagine it will prove very difficult to treat her by hand.'

Daisy bit her lip, desperately wanting relief now. He was right; there was no way she could function in such a disordered state. She needed his help. She looked up at him pleadingly, grinding her sex hard against his hand, completely unashamed of the copious wetness she knew he could feel there.

He smiled at her and began to massage the soft folds of her sex, first gently, then with more vigour. Daisy abandoned herself to the ministrations of his skilful fingers, crying out with no concern for her shameless display. She didn't know what to expect but she knew it when it came. The powerful feelings seemed to spread out from her sex, flooding her whole body. Every muscle was tensed and trembling as she hovered on the brink of ecstasy. At last she reached a peak and a series of spasms overtook her, making her scream. She clamped her legs tightly around his hand as she succumbed to the internal battering that pounded her like waves.

She went limp as the violent spasms gradually faded to a gentle pulsing. She rolled onto her side and drew her legs up to her chest, curling into a ball. She heard the doctor's voice as if from far away, addressing the room. Whatever he was saying, it had nothing to do with her. Any anxiety she had been feeling at the start of the demonstration was long gone. All she wanted now was to bask in the glow of the delicious relief.

Some time later, he helped her to her feet. The room was empty. He turned away discreetly as she dressed herself, her legs shaky from the experience. She was certain the evidence of what he had done to her was painted across her face for all to see.

'You did very well,' he said, 'and you've more than earned your fee.' He passed her the gold sovereign he had promised her.

'Thank you, sir,' she said shyly, too embarrassed to meet his eyes. She tucked the coin into her shoe and clasped her hands as she worked up the courage to ask him the question burning in her mind.

At last she spoke. 'Sir? This device you spoke of ...'

'Yes, Daisy?'

'If you ever wished to ... Well, that is to say ...' She bit her lip and forced the words out. 'Might you one day need someone for a demonstration of how it works?'

He smiled and touched her face fondly, as though he'd known all along what was in her mind.

CHAPTER TWO

Justine

It was dark by the time the coach drew up outside the house of Frankenstein. The imposing gothic façade soared above the cobbled drive, its steep gables and asymmetrical roofline carving its outline against the moonlit sky. The horses stamped their feet and snorted, breath pluming in the crisp winter air. It had been a tiring day and Frankenstein was looking forward to relaxing in his study with a glass of brandy.

Justine opened the door for him and took his coat as he stepped inside the hall. The little maid was slightly out of breath, as though she'd run to meet him at the door. Like a pet, he thought with a smile. He handed her his silver-topped walking stick and she slotted it into the rack with the others.

'Thank you, Justine,' he said. As she turned back to him, he reached up to her face, fingering a wisp of dark hair that had come loose from her mob cap. He raised his eyebrows.

She blushed and began smoothing her hair back, tucking the loose strands up under her cap. 'Sorry, sir. I was upstairs when I heard the coach. I was ... blacking the grates.'

'I see.' He took her hand and peered closely at the fingers. They were spotless. 'You can't have made a very good job of it.'

Again she blushed, lowering her head. Unable to improve on her already poor fabrication, she was silent for several seconds. He took pity on her and laughed, gently smacking the back of her hand. 'It's all right, my girl,' he said. 'There's nothing to be ashamed of. You were in my rooms again, weren't you?'

She gasped and feigned innocence. 'Sir! I –'

'You know what they say about curious little pussy-cats, don't you?'

She bit her lip, fidgeting where she stood as he tormented her, her fingers clutching the lace edges of her pinafore. He knew full well what she had been up to. What girl wouldn't be curious about the mysterious devices he kept in his locked cabinets? Justine was the one who answered the door to his lady patients, after all, and saw them out again. They were always glowing and a little dishevelled when they left. She was bound to be curious about this special treatment of his that was so popular that these

11

women came back to see him time after time. And he didn't doubt for a moment that she'd stood outside his consulting room, ear pressed to the door, eyes wide with wonder at the sounds that came from within.

He wasn't annoyed with her in the slightest, but she was so fetching in her discomfiture he found himself looking for excuses to chide her simply so he could watch her squirm. He felt himself growing hard whenever he teased her. He recalled watching the delicious battle between shame and excitement the day he had hired her, subjecting her to a thorough and completely unnecessary physical examination. What fun he'd had coaxing her out of her dress, her corset, her chemise and pantalets. But just as no man could hide the bulge in his trousers when aroused, no woman could conceal the telltale wetness. And Justine was no exception.

'The demonstration went well,' he told her breezily. Initially he'd thought of pressing Justine into service for it, knowing she'd have responded exactly as Daisy had. But then he'd thought better of it. Occasionally, students or colleagues came to the house and the girl would have a devil of a time opening the door or serving tea to men who had seen her in such a state. He had a cruel streak, but not even he could do that to his sweet little maid.

'That's good, sir,' she said, relaxing now that the subject of her snooping seemed to have been dropped. But he didn't intend to let her off the hook so easily.

'Yes, the girl was very responsive and I'm satisfied that the students are better informed now as regards the intricacies of female anatomy.'

Her cheeks blazed scarlet again and she chewed her lower lip. 'Oh.'

'Indeed, they wanted more. They wanted a demonstration of the Alleviator, but I told them it wouldn't be possible, as it was simply too big to transport.'

At that he saw her eyes flick to the door of his reception room and then quickly away again. Ah, yes, the little fish was hooked. She knew the machine by name only; she had never seen it.

'Besides,' he continued, 'I didn't think it fair to subject a girl to that kind of exhibition. It does provoke rather intense and extreme responses in a young lady and I didn't want the girl to feel at all inhibited by the public setting. In private, they can let go fully, as I'm the only one there to see.'

Justine swallowed audibly as she pretended to make some adjustment to the scattering of calling cards in the little silver salver on the hall table. 'Very thoughtful, sir,' was apparently all she could think of to say.

'So who's come calling today?' There were three cards on the salver, each bearing the name of a young lady doubtless suffering the malady he alone seemed able to treat. 'Miss Anna Fairfax, Mrs Gwendolyn Merrydale …'

'Yes, sir, they asked if you could please see them right

away. That lady –' she pointed to a familiar gilt-edged card '– said it was a matter of extreme urgency.'

'I see.'

The card Justine indicated belonged to a Mrs Sylvia Leigh-Hunt. She was a wealthy widow he'd been 'treating' for several months. She was a few years younger than his forty-two, but still a handsome woman. There was nothing at all wrong with her, but that was hardly the point. He was an expert in the art of separating rich fools from their money.

'How did the other two look?' he asked.

'Oh, Miss Fairfax was a lovely young thing,' Justine said dreamily. 'Flaxen hair, green eyes. Like a painting she was, sir.'

He nodded. 'Mm-hmm. And Mrs Merrydale?'

Justine frowned slightly and shook her head. 'I told her you weren't taking on any new patients.'

He laughed. Ah, yes, she knew her master's tastes. 'Good girl,' he said. 'You've done very well. Do you know, I think you've earned yourself a reward.'

Her eyes widened as she looked up at him, her face open and trusting and entirely innocent of what he had in mind. She may have thought Miss Fairfax was lovely, but Justine was quite a picture herself. She was twenty-three, slim and petite, sylph-like. But what he found most striking was the contrast of pale-blue eyes and dark hair. It gave her an air of mystery. He had seen her naked, of course, but he had never seen her with her hair down. She always kept it pinned up and tucked into her cap. It would fall in loose wanton waves round her shoulders if she let it down, like that of a gypsy or a wild woman.

Her delicate bone structure belied her low station and he had often toyed with the notion of dressing her as a lady and training her up. Teaching her manners, how to speak, how to walk, how to comport herself. He could see her clothed in a gown of vibrant silk, cut low across the bosom, jewels gleaming against her slender throat. He was sure she could pass for a lady given the right training. Ah, but a lady in public only. In private, he would teach her tricks that would make a whore blush.

Since entering his service, she had proven loyal and obedient. She had no family and no ties to the world outside. Until recently. In the past few weeks she had become sweet on the butcher's boy Ralph, whom she saw whenever she went to the market to run errands. He was a handsome lad, but Frankenstein knew a bounder when he saw one. He'd seen the way the boy looked at her and he'd cautioned her against giving her heart away too readily, for it was bound to get broken. Still, even the brightest girl is made foolish by love and Frankenstein determined to keep an eye on his little maid, lest she be seduced. By someone other than him.

'Would my curious little cat like to see what I keep in that locked chamber?'

A beautiful blush painted her cheeks and she fixed her eyes on the floor, where she nudged the toe of one boot against the other, in an agony of indecision. He spared her the misery of admitting her curiosity, took her by the hand and led her into the reception room. She lingered in the doorway as he withdrew a set of keys and unlocked his consulting room, then beckoned her further, as though into a sinister lair. He smiled at the thought, for in a way it was exactly that. Certain of the ladies he saw were under no illusion about what was really going on, but the majority of them had been so conditioned by prudish society as to genuinely believe there was nothing sexual in what he did to them. One day the world would catch on and his little speciality would come to an end. Until then, however, he intended to exploit it to the fullest.

Justine plucked at her skirt, nervously peering around at the cabinets and cupboards. He adjusted the gas lamp and moved deeper into the room, to the inner sanctum, the chamber in which the beast slept, awaiting another victim.

'Sir, I'm not sure I should ...'

Frankenstein returned to her and took her gently by the shoulders, offering her his most charming smile. Doubtless she feared he would persuade her out of her clothes again, a thought he couldn't deny had crossed his mind. 'Justine,' he said, 'we both know you've been in here before without my permission. Didn't I say when I hired you that I needed a girl I could trust?'

'Yes, sir.'

'Now, I don't mind that you're inquisitive, but that doesn't give you leave to snoop.'

A delicate frown creased her features and she bit her lip. 'No, sir,' she mumbled.

'I've never expressly forbidden you to come in here when I'm away – you certainly know where the spare key is kept – but I shouldn't have thought it necessary. Good little chambermaids do not go sneaking around in their master's private rooms.'

Although he spoke softly, smiling indulgently all the while, the girl was writhing in a horror of delicious embarrassment. He wondered if she could see how hard it was making him, or indeed if she had sufficient knowledge to recognise such things. Ralph had surely tried, by less eloquent means, to manoeuvre the girl into a compromising position. If so, he had clearly been unsuccessful. Such a rascal would be gone like a shot afterwards and never seen again.

'It was very naughty of you, wasn't it?'

Mortified, she couldn't meet his eyes. He was so close he was sure he could smell her arousal, soft and spicy. She trembled like a rabbit caught in a trap, vulnerable and completely available to him. The girl was so naturally submissive that the very thought of disappointing her master would be a torment for her. If he kept it up much longer, he would reduce her to tears. He caught her chin between his thumb and forefinger and lifted her head.

'But we were talking about a reward,' he said kindly. 'Weren't we?'

She relaxed at once, a sheepish grin spreading across her features. 'Yes, sir.'

'I trust you to look after my needs, so it's only fair I should trust you with my secrets as well. And I think you deserve to know what goes on. What could possibly be improper about that?'

'I just wasn't sure that Ralph would approve of his future wife knowing about – well, certain things ...'

Ah, so the scoundrel saw him as a threat, did he? Well, perhaps one seducer could recognise another, but Frankenstein was far more accomplished at this game than he was. There was no way he was going to allow that insolent pup to spoil his lovely Justine.

'I see,' he said sadly. 'So it's fine for a maid to nose around where she isn't allowed but when her master trusts her enough to show her himself ...'

Her hands flew to her mouth to stifle a little gasp of horror. 'Oh no, sir! I didn't mean ... I just ...'

'Very well,' he shrugged, returning the keys to his pocket and turning to leave. 'I had no idea you had such a low opinion of me, Justine.'

He had to suppress a grin at the miserable sniffle he

heard behind him as he walked away. If there was one thing an honest girl couldn't bear, it was the thought that she had broken someone's trust.

'Sir?' she said at last, her voice wavering.

He turned back to her, his loins twitching with the sense of imminent victory.

She offered him a meek little smile as she moved towards the door of the private chamber. 'Please forgive me, sir. I was being foolish.'

Frankenstein smiled. Sometimes it was just too easy. He unlocked the door and led her into the darkened chamber.

After a long silence, she asked, 'Is that it?'

'The Alleviator,' he said with pride. 'Indeed it is.'

He could tell from her face that it was nothing like she had imagined. How often had ladies told him they'd been expecting something huge and fearsome? A massive steam-driven automaton that would violently pound the nervous energy out of them and leave them feeling plundered? He was fascinated by the wild fancies that seemed equal parts fear and desire. What strange creatures women were, really.

'The patient lies here,' he explained, touching the padded surface of the table, 'and the motor is concealed beneath.'

Justine dropped to her knees to peer under the table, gazing at the device and trying to guess how it worked. He knew she would never ask him outright.

'Would you like to see how it works?'

She jumped as if he'd read her mind and cast her eyes down shyly, her silence all the answer he needed. It was another thing he'd learnt in his dealings with women; they so often needed the illusion of coercion or even force to ease their sense of shame. He had become a master at such games and found that the intricate manoeuvring only added to the fun.

He placed his hands around her waist and lifted her up onto the table. She uttered a little squeak of surprise but didn't protest.

'And now you must lie back,' he said, pushing her down with a hand against her breastbone.

She resisted only for a moment before letting him lower her into position. If she was surprised that he hadn't asked her to undress she didn't let on. He had, after all, assured her that it was all entirely proper. A lady didn't have to be naked to allow access and he was very careful about which ones he demanded it of. All it took was one knowing husband and the whole lucrative venture would be ruined. Today he merely wanted to give Justine a taste, enough to whet her appetite for more. He was determined that in time she would learn to ask for what she wanted.

She blinked in surprise as he gathered her skirt and raised it to her waist before she could object. But she was cowed by her earlier reluctance and, although she stiffened a little at the exposure, she lay still.

'Good girl. And now if you'll just part your legs, just a bit …'

She closed her eyes and did as she was told. Underneath she wore the customary open-seam drawers. The garment clothed each leg to the knee, but the legs were separately stitched to the drawstring at the waist, allowing for easy access to the exposed crotch. He had provided them along with her uniform, but he had treated her (and himself) to a fashionable frill of lace at the kneebands. A bit above a maid's station, but who would ever see but him? Well, perhaps that wretched Ralph …

Justine trembled as he firmly pulled her knees a little further apart. Dampness glistened like dew on the dark thatch of hair at the branching of her thighs.

'Dear me,' he said, shaking his head. 'This won't do at all.'

The little maid looked instantly alarmed, fearful she'd done something wrong. 'Sir?'

'You are not appropriately prepared.'

She blinked, not comprehending.

'All my patients must be shaved,' he explained, 'for reasons of safety and hygiene. You can hardly expect me to probe and stroke and treat the nether parts of you in anything like the detail you need if they are concealed.'

Without waiting for a response, he fetched his shaving things. Of course, the procedure wasn't necessary at all; it was just his preference. He liked to see everything.

Most women found the experience highly erotic, although naturally they tried to pretend they were merely obeying his obscure orders.

The shaving also served another purpose. It ensured that a lady would show herself to no one else, not even another physician. It was as good as a mark of ownership. In this case it would give Justine extra incentive to see that Ralph kept his hands to himself. At least until the hair grew back. Then he would have to contrive an excuse to shave her again.

Justine's eyes widened as she saw the straight razor. 'Will it hurt?' she asked.

He smiled. 'Not if you're a good girl and hold very still for me.' Then he set about daubing her with shaving soap.

She jumped a little at the first touch of the brush but after that she didn't move. He coaxed her legs wide apart and painted her sex with lather. He couldn't resist pressing the soft bristles well up against her, which elicited a little moan. Her thighs relaxed and her legs opened wider still, like the petals of a hungry flower spreading itself for the rays of the sun.

'Now I want you to be perfectly still, Justine,' he said. 'You *will* be still, won't you?'

'Yes, sir,' came the breathless whisper.

Oh yes, she was ready.

He bent over her and slowly drew the blade down over her pubic mound, carving a path through the lather. She gasped and he placed the fingers of his left hand firmly on the vulnerable pink skin he had just revealed, a silent command not to move. Gooseflesh rose on her thighs and she shivered slightly. He wiped the blade clean and swept it through another patch of foam.

This was an especially intimate ritual among the many in his repertoire and he took his time over it. He loved the entire process of unveiling. For him it was more art than science. As the blade rasped and the dark curls fell away he was treated to a sight few men ever got to see – a woman's sex, wholly uncovered and exposed for his eyes, his hands, his instruments. The ultimate submissive offering.

Holding her skin taut, he slid the razor up each inner thigh, angling each stroke in to the centre point of her sex. He carefully trimmed away everything that might obscure his view. Nothing must remain but her perfect mound, silky and smooth.

It was over far too quickly, both for him and for Justine, whose breathing had grown fast and shallow. Once, she had lifted her head to peer down at what he was doing, then blushed and looked away, clasping her hands at her breast. With all the hair removed he could easily see the reason for her embarrassment: she was exceedingly wet. It was all he could do not to dip his finger inside. Instead he made do with towelling her dry and dabbing at her in such a way as to produce more of those charming little gasps and sighs.

'There,' he said triumphantly. 'That's much better.'

She glanced down and her mouth fell open in mute surprise as she saw herself clearly for the first time.

'Now we can proceed.'

He pressed a button at the end of the table and the engine whirred to life, rumbling beneath it. Justine jumped a little at the vibrations and then began to smile.

'It's very pleasant, sir,' she said. 'Like riding on the train.'

He smiled at her naïveté. 'Oh, that's not all.'

He allowed himself a final lingering look at her before proceeding to the next step. The business end of the machine was a small device, about the size and shape of an egg, attached to a hinged metal arm. He lowered the buzzing attachment and rested it against Justine's bare sex. She gave a little cry of surprise as the powerful vibrations began to pulse through her. No, she hadn't been expecting that. None of them ever knew what they were in for.

Adopting his most soothing voice, he told her to relax, to submit to the device. Her face took on a familiar dreamy cast as her body realised what was happening and she sank into the pleasure. Everything was centred on that one small part of her and it quickly became her whole world.

How delightful it was to watch the play of emotions across a woman's face the first time she felt those vibrations! Naturally, some ladies were too repressed to let go, despite his constant reassurances. There was no impropriety, he was a medical man, it was all for their own good. Sometimes none of it could break through the barrier. Such women seemed determined to suffer, to deny themselves pleasure, even in the form of alleged clinical relief.

Justine was an excellent subject. He had tricked her into it so there need be no guilt on her part. And she clearly had a sensual nature; shaving her had shown him that quite plainly. Now she was rocking her hips back and forth to get the most out of the experience. In time, he could introduce her to other devices, other pleasures. He had no doubt that she would prove a very eager pupil.

As he sensed her nearing the peak, he turned a knob to increase the speed. Her fingers clutched the edges of the table and she raised her hips, forcing her pelvis roughly against the source of the pleasure until she gave a wild cry as the wave of spasms overtook her. Then she collapsed, gasping and panting, dazed and spent.

Smiling, Frankenstein shut off the machine and tidied up while she recovered, her legs still splayed, her face flushed and blissful. When she still hadn't moved after several minutes, he gently drew her skirt down, reluctantly concealing her charms. That seemed to wake her up. She covered her face with her hands as though trying to force her smile into hiding.

'Well, my girl, I trust you feel suitably rewarded?'

She nodded, amazement painting her features. 'Oh sir, I've never felt such … It was …'

'I know. It cures all manner of ills. Now perhaps you understand why the treatment is so popular.'

'I do indeed, sir. I had no idea!'

He helped her up and she stumbled a little as she tried to stand. It was another sight he relished. After soaring with euphoria, they found it a challenge to return to solid ground. Ah, such power he had! In some bygone era he would have been the village's medicine man, the wise and mysterious enchanter to whom all the women were in thrall.

Justine gazed blankly around the room, still lost to the unfamiliar sensations. He'd awakened every nerve ending in her body, assaulting her with pleasure and now she seemed overwhelmed.

He decided to give her the evening off, even though he knew she might waste it on the butcher's boy. In fact, Frankenstein rather hoped Ralph would see a change in his little conquest and realise that he was a poor second to whatever her master had done to her.

All in all, it had been a successful day and Frankenstein was delighted with the progress he'd made with Justine. He led her back to the hallway and smiled as she made her unsteady way upstairs.

His eye fell on the salver and he pocketed the calling

cards, doubly pleased that his list of patients was growing. Some gossipy lady must have put the word out. At this rate he would have the most successful practice in all of London. Not that any of that mattered to him; it was the money the practice brought in that was important. By the end of the month he should have enough to buy a crucial piece of equipment for the rooftop laboratory. Then he could bury himself in his *real* work. His life's work.

CHAPTER THREE

A Curious Visitor

'Sir? There's a gentleman here to see you.'

Frankenstein looked up from his desk, frowning. He didn't like being disturbed when he was working and Justine would never have dreamt of it if the man hadn't been so persuasive. She opened her mouth to explain but the visitor brushed past her and strode breezily into the room. To her surprise, her master's face broke into a broad smile.

'Pretorius,' he exclaimed. 'How delightful! I never thought to see you again, old friend!'

The visitor had introduced himself to Justine at the door as *Doctor* Pretorius, so she assumed he worked at the hospital. He was a handsome man with a soft, mellifluous voice and a pleasant demeanour and he wore a coat of extravagant purple velvet. Indeed, he had quite charmed his way into the house, despite Justine's insistence that her master did not like to be disturbed.

'My dear girl,' he'd said, 'I can assure you he'll want to see *me*.'

And so she'd smiled sheepishly and let him in, hoping he was right and that Frankenstein wouldn't tell her off for interrupting him. It was the only time he was ever cross with her. He spent hours up in his rooftop laboratory working with strange contraptions that she assumed he must intend for use in his practice and he got so consumed by his work that sometimes he even forgot to eat. She'd made the mistake of disturbing him one time when he was up there and he'd smashed a glass bottle on the floor and shouted at her to get out. Afterwards, he had brought her a little cake to make amends but she'd never dared to enter the laboratory again. Tonight, however, he was in his downstairs study. If Pretorius had wanted her to bother her master in the laboratory she'd have certainly stood her ground.

Pretorius set his case down on the floor and the two men shook hands warmly. There was clearly nothing more for her to do here, so she bobbed an awkward curtsey which neither man noticed and slipped quietly out of the room, closing the door behind her.

She listened at the keyhole for a few moments but they were drinking brandy and reminiscing about old times, nothing of interest to her. Apparently they had known one another at medical school and she gathered from the conversation that Pretorius was an expert on something called 'nymphomania'. He said that his practice had been successful enough to allow him to retire early and devote himself entirely to research. Then there was a lot of technical talk that Justine couldn't follow. She soon grew bored with eavesdropping and wandered off to the kitchen, where it was warm.

Her legs still ached from her exertions the other day, when her master had shown her the Alleviator. And shaved her. She blushed to recall it, although the memory excited her too. She wasn't sure whether it was wrong to feel that way, but surely something that made one feel so good couldn't be bad. After all, the procedure was meant to be a sort of therapy, wasn't it? And ladies of good standing flocked here to the house and paid handsomely to receive it. In any case, he'd reassured her that there was no impropriety and she trusted him completely.

Justine was well aware how lucky she was. She knew of maids who toiled day and night for far less than she earned. Her duties were very light by comparison with stories she heard of other houses.

Indeed, Ralph had told her just the other night of one house he knew of where the maids were all got from the workhouse. He said that the master of that house was a high court judge who was on a crusade to reform 'fallen women' by his own unorthodox methods, which included tying them down and birching them when they displeased him. But that wasn't even the worst of it, according to Ralph.

The judge had a special room in his house where the miscreant had to wait until he came to see her, to reprimand her for whatever she'd done wrong, and then she had to ask him very nicely to punish her. Ralph seemed to know the names of all these unfortunate maids and all the details of the elaborate disciplinary rituals they were subjected to, as though he'd somehow managed to insinuate himself into the house and watch. He had seemed especially fascinated by the plight of a girl called Sally, who had stolen some sherry from the butler's pantry one evening and been made an example of before the entire household.

'The judge made her wear a special uniform after that,' he'd said, 'with her skirts pinned up and her drawers removed entirely. So the other girls could see the stripes he'd painted on her arse and know that they'd suffer the same fate if they got out of line.'

Justine had blanched at the thought of being whipped for such trifling offences as spilling tea or dropping a fork while laying the table, to say nothing of the added humiliation for a crime like stealing. Which of course Justine would never commit. But Ralph had seemed peculiarly intrigued by the whole business. He had asked Justine if Dr Frankenstein was ever so strict with her and what happened to her when she displeased him. He didn't seem to want to believe her when she assured him that her master was nothing like that terrible judge, that he was kind and gentle and very forgiving of her faults. He had never raised a hand to her and she held him in very high esteem. He was a perfect gentleman.

Something in Ralph's expression had disquieted her. He almost seemed disappointed, as though he'd *wanted* to hear tales of harsh discipline at her master's hands. Later he'd tried to get her to lift her skirts and show him her quim and her eyes had widened with fear, which only seemed to confirm what he suspected about Frankenstein's cruelty.

'Come on, Sally, let me see the marks,' he pleaded, his voice low and hoarse.

'Sally?'

'Sorry, I meant Justine of course. It's only that I was just telling you about Sally and ... Oh, let me see. Just a peek.'

Justine didn't dare let him see what her master *had* done to her, however pleasant it had been. The embarrassment would have killed her. So instead she put him off with chaste indignation and he became annoyed and called her a tease.

But she didn't want to be a bad girl like the kind who ended up in the workhouse to be spirited away by cruel judges. She would be happy to show him everything on their wedding night. Justine was a good girl and she was determined to remain so. Ralph had stewed for a while and then cooled off. And if he was a little less enthusiastic when he said he would call on her again in a few days, well, that was fair enough. Once married, she would never deny him. She knew he would understand.

Justine wasn't worldly wise but she did know that men had needs of a kind that women couldn't understand. Her friend Daisy had told her all about it. Once, she had even shown Justine some drawings in a book, when her father had left her in charge of the bookshop for the day. Now *there* was a girl who was overworked! And she wasn't even a maid – just a shop girl. Justine felt sorry for her, shut up in that dusty, gloomy shop all day, never allowed out for a walk in the park. Justine's life was one of leisure by comparison.

Her thoughts turned from Daisy back to Ralph. Perhaps by the time she saw him again, the shaved hair would have grown back. Dr Frankenstein had said it shouldn't take very long. Perhaps then she would let Ralph see. Just a little peek. Surely there could be no harm in that. Not if it was true love.

Justine warmed herself by the stove for a while before becoming curious once more about the unexpected visitor. Dr Pretorius had had a strange sort of case with him. At first she'd taken it for a medical bag but now that she thought about it, it had looked more like a birdcage under a cloth. Yes, and hadn't she heard a little squeak of some kind when he set it down?

Knowing full well that it was none of her business, but also knowing that there were unlikely to be any consequences if she were caught (no matter what Ralph wanted to believe), she tiptoed back to the study door and crouched down to peer through the keyhole. Dr Pretorius was just unveiling the case and she was right; it *was* a cage! But what it contained was certainly no bird.

'What on earth –?' Frankenstein gasped, staring down at what Justine first took to be a doll.

Pretorius beamed with pride as he unlocked the door of the cage and coaxed the little creature out. 'I call her Cleo.'

Justine clapped a hand over her mouth to stifle her cry of shock. What emerged from the cage was either a living doll or an extraordinarily tiny woman. Only a few inches high, she wore a filmy white dress that revealed more than it concealed. Her feet were bare and her long red hair cascaded down her back. She crept hesitantly towards Pretorius's hand before climbing into it. He lifted her up and held her out for Frankenstein to see.

Her master shook his head in bewilderment and Pretorius gave a good-natured little laugh as he stroked the woman's flowing red hair with a fingertip.

'She's a homunculus,' he explained, 'or homuncula, if you prefer. She is, after all, most assuredly female.'

'But where did you … How did you …?'

Pretorius moved closer to the fire, presumably to warm the tiny creature. In doing so he provided Justine with an even better view of the proceedings. She could see that Cleo was quite lovely. Her minute hands and feet were exquisitely formed, as were the delicate features of her face. Around her neck she wore a gleaming gold band, very like a collar one would put on a pet. Justine was certain she could make out the glittering of a tiny gold chain attached to it.

'Isn't she splendid?'

Frankenstein simply nodded. He seemed quite unable to speak.

'You see,' Pretorius said with a touch of pride, 'while you were skulking about in graveyards in the dead of night looking for specimens, I went to the very source of life itself. This little pet of mine was created wholly by me, grown in my laboratory as one might grow and tend a rare flower. Of course, in this case the flower has been given a rather special diet of aphrodisiacs. It is a formula I've been perfecting for years.'

Cleo wrapped her arms around Pretorius's thumb as Frankenstein bent down for a closer look. She drew back as he reached out a finger to poke her.

'There's no need to be afraid,' Pretorius told her. 'Despite her fragile appearance she is surprisingly robust. And ever so ... talented.'

Frankenstein blinked at him for a moment and then he broke into a hearty laugh. 'You old devil! Are you telling me you're corrupting this poor creature?'

35

Pretorius snorted. 'My dear chap, she is no innocent maiden. She is as nature – and science – made her. Wholly in thrall to her baser urges and refreshingly uncontaminated by the strictures of this prudish society in which we live.'

Justine blinked in confusion, not understanding a word of what they were saying. If they meant that the fairy-like woman was some kind of animal, she didn't understand why Frankenstein found it so amusing. And what was that about graveyards?

'Is she perfectly formed?' Frankenstein asked.

'See for yourself. Have you a magnifying glass?'

'I have.' He went to fetch it from the desk while Pretorius set Cleo down on the low table, between their brandy glasses. She could easily have fitted inside one. He whispered something to her that Justine couldn't hear. But suddenly Cleo was undressing. She slithered out of the sheer garment and stood naked in the flickering light from the fire.

Frankenstein returned with a large magnifying glass and proceeded to look her over in detail, prodding her and turning her this way and that, while Pretorius looked on, smiling. Cleo seemed quite unconcerned by this intimate attention but it made Justine blush to the roots of her hair. The tiny woman did as she was directed, bending over, spreading her legs, displaying herself in a variety of positions. It almost looked as though she was enjoying herself, adding little flourishes to her movements. At Pretorius's instruction she caressed her breasts, pressing them together to accentuate their fullness as she smiled up at both men.

'You see she has no reservations about her sexuality,' Pretorius said. 'She is as free as you or I.'

Frankenstein quirked an eyebrow at his friend and grinned. 'Free?'

'Well, of course not "free" in the sense that she may go anywhere she likes. She is my creation and she therefore belongs to me. Don't you, my pet?'

Cleo stood on tiptoe and stretched her hands up to her master. She bounced happily on her heels by way of response, like a puppy.

'But she is happy. And she keeps me happy. Her arms and legs are just the right length to fit round – well, I'm sure you can picture the scene. Naturally, I cannot have her in the normal way, but I'm working on a device that will allow me to alter her size at will.'

Frankenstein laughed, shaking his head in disbelief. 'You were always the more decadent of the two of us.'

'Yes,' Pretorius said. He took a sip of brandy and his eyes glinted in the firelight. 'And just imagine what we might achieve together, Victor! Your first experiment was not, after all, a complete success.'

'You are too kind, old friend. A wretched failure would be more accurate.'

Rose de Fer

'Whatever became of the creature?'

'I never found his body. My old laboratory was completely incinerated, along with all the equipment. It has taken me years to replace everything but I'm nearly ready to begin again.'

'And this time,' Pretorius said, as though making a grand announcement, 'you shall have my help. Together we will achieve goals undreamt of by the little minds of men who dare to call themselves scientists.' As he spoke he swept Cleo up into his hand and slipped her into his coat pocket. Her head peeked out and she gazed contentedly up at Pretorius.

Justine pressed her thighs together, suddenly struck by the fantasy of being small enough to fit inside a man's pocket. She thought of the fun she could have with ordinary objects. For some reason the image of a butterfly collection came to her and she pictured herself spread and displayed behind glass, one of many tiny specimens to be admired.

What would Ralph think if she were suddenly only six inches high? He could bathe her in a teacup and dry her with his handkerchief. And she could wrap her tiny naked arms around his cock and not be ashamed to let him peer at her charms through a magnifying glass. Her face burned as she imagined all the possibilities.

Pretorius raised his brandy glass to make a toast and Justine decided it was a good time to slip away. She had

38

no idea what the two men were talking about or what experiment had gone so horribly wrong for Frankenstein. It must have been before she entered his service. But what little she *had* understood, not to mention the extraordinary reality of Cleo, had set her mind spinning with what her master in his professional capacity would call hysteria. She knew a way to relieve it herself but she didn't dare. If he should ring for her and she arrived looking flushed and dishevelled before them both ... Well, the possibility was too embarrassing to consider.

As she crept back down the hallway, she heard their glasses clink together. It seemed to herald the beginning of a new world.

CHAPTER FOUR

The Perfect Opportunity

A few days later, Frankenstein stood in his laboratory admiring the water tank. It had taken eight men to manoeuvre it up the stairs and into the laboratory but now that it was in place it seemed as though it had always been there. A heated pipe had slowly filled it with snowmelt from the roof. Now it awaited an occupant.

Just imagine what we might achieve together, Victor!

Frankenstein was in no doubt about the genius of Pretorius; the tiny Cleo was proof of that. She was also a reminder that the creation of strange new life was within his grasp. But strange new life of a more appealing kind than that wretched first experiment. From the very start the monster had resented its creator, rebelling against every instruction and every attempt to civilise it. Where he had gone wrong was in using a male subject. Females were far more submissive and malleable. Not to mention physically weaker and therefore easier to control. Pretorius's homuncula had all the qualities her creator had desired in a woman: beauty, obedience and – perhaps most importantly – a powerful sexual appetite. With his friend's help, Frankenstein would create his own perfect woman. He could almost see her floating in the tank now, drifting like the promise of triumph.

'Victor? Is anything the matter?'

He shook himself out of his reverie, surprised for a moment to find himself in his bedroom and not the laboratory. Sylvia Leigh-Hunt stood before him in her red silk corset and petticoats, frozen in the act of undressing. The widow's face bore a faintly wounded expression.

'Forgive me, my dear,' he said, reminding himself whose patronage he was indebted to for quite a lot of his equipment. He arranged his features into a lover's smile and kissed her hand. 'I have taken a strange fancy into my head and I was merely wondering whether it might shock you too terribly if I were to suggest it.'

Sylvia's face brightened at the prospect of a new game and Frankenstein was again struck by her beauty. The years had been kind to her, and her wealthy husband's untimely demise had been kinder still, for mourning truly became her. An alluring woman, her face bore few signs of her fortyish years, and her black garments and crepe veil suited her surprisingly well. He supposed it was somewhat perverse of him to find her widow's weeds

erotic but then, what was his entire practice if not insti-
tutionalised perversion? Most of his lady patients were
innocent of what was really going on but Sylvia was a
shrewd woman who knew a good thing when she found
it. It had taken Frankenstein several 'treatment sessions'
to realise that neither was fooling the other. Now there
was little pretence about why she really came to see him.

'What did you have in mind?' she asked.

He nodded towards the chair where she had discarded
her outer garments. 'I'd quite like to see you in your veil.'

She looked puzzled. 'Again, you mean? But I always
wear it when I come.'

Frankenstein shook his head, a suggestive grin
spreading over his face. 'That's what I want to see: you
wearing it when you come.' He emphasised the last word
so there could be no mistaking his intent.

Sylvia blushed like a maid half her age and giggled
behind her hand. 'Oh, you are too wicked!' she cried.

She made a little show of wiggling her peachy
bottom as she crossed the room to fetch the black veil.
Frankenstein admired her figure as she stood silhouetted
before the window. She was a committed tight-lacer,
and her waist measured an astonishing sixteen inches.
The sight of her body mercilessly laced and bound was
peculiarly arousing. Personally, Frankenstein wished that
more women would submit their bodies to such rigours.
He was fascinated by the extremes they were willing

to endure for the sake of fashion. The corset not only pinched her waist; it exaggerated the swell of her bosom and hips, creating the dramatic hourglass shape that dress reformers and fainthearted doctors claimed would lead to madness or even death.

Pretorius was quite correct about the small minds of the scientific and medical community. Surely even the most callow student could see that a corset was far less dangerous to a woman's body than pregnancy and childbirth, which killed so many. Despite strident objections to the practice, there had never been a single documented case of injury or illness attributed to tight-lacing. And if the ignorant fools who called themselves men of science could be so misguided about something as inconsequential as female undergarments, how could they hope to understand the mysteries of life and death? No, it was for men like him and Pretorius to show them the way. And show them they would!

Sylvia slithered out of her petticoats and, now clad only in her corset and veil, turned back to Frankenstein. The black netting fell past her face and over her shoulders, dramatically offsetting the red silk of the corset. Beneath her respectable dress she always wore the lavish colours of a whore.

Frankenstein approached her, admiring the scandalous sight of her. He stirred his finger in the air and she obliged him by turning in a slow circle so he could inspect her.

The edge of the veil came to the top of her bottom, accentuating the roundness of her cheeks and the deep dimples he found so charming. As she completed her turn, he noted the fuzzy triangle of hair just beginning to obscure her sex. Had it really been so long since he'd seen her last? He kept her shaved as they both enjoyed the process and she had no other admirers, but he had been neglecting his duties, both professional and personal, since Pretorius's visit and the subsequent new preparations in the laboratory.

'You're a vision,' he told her, meaning it.

She lifted the black veil like a ghostly bride and beamed happily at him, basking in the compliment.

The sight of her waist, so cruelly whittled by the scarlet corset, inflamed him even more. He often fucked her while she was still laced – she had several corsets from the finest makers in London and Paris – but today he wanted to see her naked but for the veil. He caught her by her tiny waist and pivoted her so she was facing away from him. Then he firmly guided her forwards until her hands rested on the seat of the chair. He gathered her cheeks in his hands, kneading them as he told her how he intended to have her. She shuddered under his touch, sighing at each indignity he proposed.

He deftly untied the knot at the back of her corset and began loosening the laces bit by bit. He took his time, prolonging the act. He actually preferred lacing her *into* the torturous garments. Her little gasps as he pulled the laces tighter always made his cock ache with need. More than once he had had to stop what he was doing and plunge himself into her again before he could complete the process.

When he had loosened the laces enough, he turned her around and unhooked the busk, smiling at her ecstatic inhalation as the stays fell away and she could breathe fully again. Her smooth and creamy skin was welted from the pressure of the corset and he trailed his fingers over the indentations made by the whalebone, causing her to tremble. In spite of their ample size, her breasts were high and firm and he bent his head to kiss each stiffening pink nipple.

Sylvia's legs trembled and threatened to give way as he slipped his hand between them, pressing his palm up against her sex. He teased her clit with his thumb and then with a finger he tapped the puckered hole of her arse. She whimpered softly at the wordless promise.

He tugged the veil back down over her face. Then he stepped away to admire the lewd spectacle: a naked woman in a mourning veil, flushed with desire and eager to be ravished. And her husband not even dead four months.

He nodded towards the bed and she went to it and sat down. On the nightstand was a vase of fresh flowers. Sylvia removed one long-stemmed white blossom and lay on the bed, holding the flower against her veiled chest.

Blood surged in his cock and his need to relieve himself became acute. He swept the edge of the veil away from her sex and roughly parted her thighs. Sylvia let out a little gasp and then he was angling himself into her. She cried out, clutching at him as he entered her forcefully and began to hammer her with the casual violence of unrestrained lust. Her body yielded to him at once. The flower was crushed between them.

He wasn't usually so rough. But the possibilities reawakened by Pretorius had fuelled the passion within him to control and conquer. He would learn the secret of life and master it. In the meantime he would master Sylvia, who was gazing at him in startled wonderment, both loving and fearing his sudden brutality.

With none of his usual finesse he seized her breasts, mauling them through the stiff material of the veil. Sylvia gasped and threw her head back, reaching above her to take hold of the carved headboard. She arched her back, offering herself to him and he responded by digging his fingers into her skin through the black mesh. She lay beneath, writhing like a creature caught in a net. The veil tore easily, exposing the reddened skin of her breasts. He fell on them, licking, sucking and biting her nipples, while she moaned and thrashed under his savage kisses.

He was right on the verge of a powerful climax when he forced himself to slow his strokes. He wasn't ready yet. Sylvia looked up at him, her mouth open to express her disappointment when he grabbed her around the waist and flipped her over.

'All fours,' he said, hoisting her into position.

Sylvia gave a little squeak of surprise but obeyed him instantly, her knees trembling. Frankenstein took up his position behind her and noted with a wicked thrill the way the remains of the veil trailed down over her back. With one brutal thrust he was inside her again, fucking her mercilessly and delivering an occasional slap to her bottom as though she were some magnificent horse he was riding. Sylvia clung to the headboard, crying out with complete abandon under his onslaught until she reached a noisy, shuddering climax.

She collapsed forwards into the pillows, panting, but Frankenstein kept her hips well up and continued to pummel her until he felt his own climax building. Then, with a last glance at the image of the ravished widow in her defiled veil, he emptied himself into her in sharp hot jets.

Afterwards, he lay on his back, dazed, as Sylvia curled next to him, purring with satisfaction.

'You've never been like that before,' she marvelled.

He didn't know what to say to that. They passed a companionable silence and then he said, 'I fear your veil is ruined.'

She shrugged. 'I have another at home. Although if this is what it does to you I may need to buy more.'

He laughed. 'I think that's a fine idea.'

They lay together for a while, basking. From outside came a faraway rumbling and Sylvia got up and went to the window. She peered out at the darkening sky and heaved a sigh.

'There's a storm brewing,' she said. 'How strange. Can it really rain when it's as cold as this?'

'I think the weather makes its own rules,' Frankenstein said, admiring the play of firelight over her shapely form.

She plucked her corset from the heap of clothes and began loosening the laces so she could put it on. 'I should go,' she said, 'or else I shall be stranded here.'

He smiled as he watched her. If she thought they were finished, she was in for a surprise, for he hadn't forgotten his silent promise to bugger her.

Sylvia slung the corset around her back and leant forwards, drawing it closed. She gathered her breasts into the front and fastened the hooks down the middle. Then she turned to Frankenstein, holding out the laces with an inviting expression.

He felt his cock twitch at the prospect of buggering her in her corset. Lacing her and moulding her body into his preferred shape would be all he needed to make him ready to take her.

Sylvia gripped the bedpost and took one final deep breath before expelling all the air from her lungs. As soon as she did Frankenstein pulled the laces tight, instantly constricting the corset by two inches. He waited a few seconds and then tugged them again, drawing the stays in a little more. Already her waist had shrunk dramatically. He took his time, enjoying the gradual process as much as the steady swelling of his cock in anticipation of having her arse. When at last the corset closed at the back, he tied the ends of the laces together and turned the dishevelled Sylvia to face him.

She saw the expression on his face at once and she chewed her lip, blushing. It was the only sexual act that embarrassed her, which only enhanced the appeal for Frankenstein. He loved nothing more than seducing a flustered woman into doing something she secretly wanted to do but couldn't bring herself to admit to.

'Now, Sylvia,' he said, adopting a gentle but authoritative tone. It was all he needed to say.

She lowered her head demurely and moved to the side of the bed, where she bent down and placed her elbows on the mattress. He slipped two fingers inside her sex and swirled them around in her wetness, enjoying her soft moans and the movement of her hips. But if she thought she could entice him to fuck her again normally instead of buggering her, she was mistaken. Whether in his bedroom or in his consulting room, he was the one in charge.

He withdrew his fingers and caressed the puckered rosebud of her anus, moistening it with her own juices. Then he gently slipped one finger inside to prepare her.

Sylvia gasped and instantly tightened around it but he stroked her and whispered to her until she relaxed enough to accommodate a second finger. When he had managed a third he knew she was ready.

With her hair disarranged and her veil in tatters he felt like a proper villain as he stood behind her and spread her cheeks apart. He pressed the head of his cock against the tiny opening, enjoying her shudder of anticipation. Then he slowly eased himself inside, an inch at a time, until he was buried in her arse. She moaned with pleasure as he began to slide in and out. Each time he filled her she clenched tightly around him, the tiny ring squeezing his cock tighter than any woman's cunt could. It was the rudest of delights, far more deviant than any of the aberrations he regularly enjoyed with his patients.

He gripped Sylvia's corseted waist, his fingers meeting around her. Sylvia tossed her head, uttering breathless little gasps and sighs, unable to pretend any longer that she was above such scandalous behaviour. And as he thrust himself in, deeper and harder, he slipped one hand around her front. She moaned as he pressed his fingers against her clit and rotated his wrist to give her the stimulation he knew she was craving.

It wasn't long before she reached another shattering climax, screaming into the bedclothes. As she came he slid his finger inside her wet cunt, intensifying her orgasm. He loved the sensation of her sex pulsing around his finger, especially as the overwhelming pleasure also caused her anus to contract around his cock. He finished seconds later with a long blissful moan, emptying himself into her bottom while she was still lost in the throes of her own ecstasy.

* * *

Sylvia left some time later, her legs unsteady and her hair in disarray, her veil destroyed. Her coachman didn't bat an eye as he handed her into the carriage. By now he was quite used to collecting her in such condition.

Exhausted from the evening's debauchery, Frankenstein was relaxing in his study when there came a sudden pounding at the front door. He waited for Justine to answer it, listening for Pretorius's voice. Surely no one else would call so late. Or be so insistent.

But he heard nothing from the direction of the front door and when the pounding began again he heaved a sigh and went to answer it himself. Two shabbily dressed men stood on the porch, their breath steaming in the frigid night air. The younger of the two held a large object bundled in a horse blanket.

The older one bowed his head and removed his woolly cap. 'So sorry to disturb you this late, sir, but we didn't know where else to bring her. We would have gone to the hospital only the lass in the bookshop said she lived here. Very tore up, she was. Said the girl was her dearest friend.'

'What are you talking about?' Frankenstein asked, not without some annoyance.

The man cast a sorrowful glance at the bundle his companion held in his arms. 'It's a story all too common, I'm afraid,' he said. 'Seems her heart was broke by some young ruffian. Run off with one of the maids from Judge Stanforth's house, so he did. So she flung herself in the river.'

Frankenstein's heart sank as he realised what must have happened. Justine, poor, trusting girl, had been forsaken by her beloved Ralph. Yes, a tragedy indeed. Now he would never get to savour the full range of her charms.

'Well, what do you expect me to do about it?' he asked gruffly.

The men exchanged a glance. 'Well, sir, it's just that my son and me – we seen some shifty characters down by the docks and we know as how there are some disreputable folk in the city ...' He broke off as though he were afraid to speak the word.

'Resurrectionists,' the son said at last.

'That's right, Joe. Body snatchers. We seen 'em chipping away at the ice before, searching for the poor souls what have met their end in them waters. The river's half frozen, you see, sir.'

The ice.

'It's good business,' he continued, 'for them as take money for selling unspoilt bodies to medical men.'

The man hesitated a moment too long and Frankenstein was on to their game. Medical men like they assumed him to be. 'Shameful practice,' he said, feigning disapproval.

'Anyway, we didn't like to see such a lovely little thing end up in the wrong hands, if you follow me, sir.'

Frankenstein produced a warm, sympathetic smile for him. 'Of course not. You've done the right thing. Please bring her inside. I'll take care of her.'

They bore their sad burden into the house with genuine care and Frankenstein found himself curiously touched by their gentleness. She was only a chambermaid, after all. One they expected to be rewarded for delivering.

He wanted her in the laboratory but he didn't want the men to see any of the equipment. It would only lead to gossip and unwanted attention. So instead he led them into the consulting room and had them lay her body out on the examining table. The father unwrapped her and made a great show of regret over retrieving the blanket.

'She won't be needing it to keep warm,' he said, 'and Lord knows we've few enough blankets as it is. It's a cold night.' He performed an elaborate shudder by way of demonstration.

Frankenstein ignored him and gazed at Justine. Her pale face bore a dusting of frost and her dress was stiffened with ice. Lightning flickered outside the windows and it was all he could do to restrain a smile.

At last he turned to the men. 'I want to thank you for your kindness,' he said grandly. He withdrew a handful of coins and pressed them into the father's hand. 'For your trouble.'

The man had the good grace to act surprised, as though he hadn't expected to be paid for his efforts. 'That's very generous of you, sir,' he said with an obsequious little bow. 'Very generous indeed.' He glanced back at Justine and shook his head sorrowfully. 'So tragic. Just like a little angel she looks.'

Frankenstein's lip curled ever so slightly, a secret smile. Yes, he thought. An angel. And with his help, she would soon take flight.

CHAPTER FIVE

Justine Unbound

He had stripped her of her sodden garments and wrapped her completely in bandages. Her slight frame, her head and each individual limb. Now she drifted in the freezing water as though asleep, her ghostly image distorted by the thin crust of ice that had formed on the surface.

Through the open skylight a long wire trailed from the lightning rod on the roof down into the tank. The storm had been threatening violence all evening; it was only a matter of time.

Despite the icy draught from the open skylight, Frankenstein was sweating. He rolled up his sleeves as he fiddled with dials and knobs, feeling powerless. All his specialised scientific equipment seemed superfluous now. He was at the mercy of the lightning. And so was Justine. If it struck it would awaken her, and the chemicals Pretorius had prepared would form her character. All his years of research and preparation suddenly seemed unnecessary when all that was required now was a simple, albeit powerful, force of nature. He felt obsolete.

The clouds rumbled with intent, bringing with them a flicker of light from above.

'It's coming,' Pretorius said, his eyes shining with mad delight as he peered up at the skylight. 'It's as though the gods approve of our ambition.'

Frankenstein didn't spare a glance for the weather churning above their heads. Instead he watched the body in the tank. The girl's arms floated loose and graceful in the water, as though she might rise and drift away like a spirit.

Pretorius was remarkably composed but Frankenstein could scarcely contain his excitement. Or his anxiety. He caught sight of his reflection in the glass of the tank and started: he looked like a madman. Disgustedly, he smoothed back his wild, windblown hair. Outside the storm howled and he heard the roof slates chattering in the fierce gusts. A small shower of snow flurried down from there and he took it as a sign. Something was about to happen. He dared not even blink now lest he miss any part of the magnificent event.

'Strike, damn you,' he muttered.

As though obeying his will, there came a terrific crack of thunder and he heard a shout from Pretorius as a jagged streak of lightning leapt in the sky. The dangling wire thrashed like a snake as the current passed through it into the tank. In the water Justine stiffened and arched backwards, all her limbs rigid. She held the pose, quivering, for several interminable seconds. Then she was still.

Frankenstein released the breath he had been holding. He could see no movement to indicate life. No curling of the fingers, no turning of the head, no attempt to draw breath. His hands clenched into fists at his sides as he cast his eyes up towards the black square of the skylight in dismay.

'It's only beginning,' Pretorius reassured him. 'There's still a chance.'

And then it happened.

With a thunderclap that made both men jump the sky blazed again with light and the wire rippled like a whip. Once more Justine writhed in the water and this time there was something deliberate in her movements, something human. Her bandaged hands clawed at the ice above her, finally punching through to clutch at the air.

With feverish excitement Frankenstein cried, 'She's alive!'

As soon as the charge had dissipated he knocked the wire aside, out of the tank. He plunged his arms into the frigid water and Pretorius assisted him in lifting the struggling girl out of the tank. They set her gently on her feet and guided her into the centre of the room. The wet bandages steamed in the warm laboratory. Water pooled at her feet and she stirred, turning her bandaged head from side to side and groping blindly with her hands.

The two men stared at one another for a moment. Then they began carefully to unwrap her. The cold wet bandages fell away like the silken wrappings of a cocoon to reveal inch after inch of flawless porcelain skin. Icy fingers grasped at Frankenstein's coat as he unwound the strips of gauze from the girl's arms, forcing himself to take his time, to savour the moment. He peeled away the binding from each exquisite hand, admiring each perfectly formed finger.

Pretorius stood behind her, unwinding a long coil of bandage from her waist. Frankenstein took her elbow and held her steady, watching in amazement as his creation was slowly revealed. Her body had suffered no damage. It was perfect. *She* was perfect. Like a statue coming to life in a sculptor's studio. He reached out to touch her pale thighs, her small round breasts, the delicate mound of her sex. She trembled at his touch, but did not jump or pull away. Only her head remained to be unveiled and Frankenstein hesitated, glancing at Pretorius.

With a grand gesture, Pretorius stepped aside.

Frankenstein touched her covered face with tenderness and smiled when Justine stretched out one bare arm to touch his in return, her fingers exploring the contours of his cheeks, mouth and nose. He gently returned her arm to her side and gave it a firm squeeze which she seemed to understand as a command to be still. Then he stripped away the final bandage.

Her long dark hair fell, wet and steaming, about her shoulders and she lifted her head as he unwound the last length of gauze. Her blue eyes gleamed like jewels in the gaslight as she peered around her without blinking. She was nothing like his first creation, that awkward creature that had stumbled and staggered in its first moments of life. The movement of her head was graceful and fluid, like the water in which she had floated for so long. She fixed him with a piercing, curious gaze and for a moment he was unnerved by the intensity of her stare. It was like being watched by a predator.

'She's alive,' Frankenstein said again, this time in an awed whisper.

Pretorius laughed softly. 'She's *yours*.'

'Yours,' Justine echoed. Her voice was low and husky, not at all the sweet girlish tone he remembered.

'Justine,' said Frankenstein. 'Do you know who I am?'

She cocked her head curiously, the way an animal might respond to an interesting noise. There was no recognition in her face and yet her eyes burned with a ferocious passion. It unnerved him.

Then she glanced down at herself, at her lithe naked form. Despite having been submerged in the icy water for hours, she seemed completely unaffected by the cold. Her skin had taken on an unearthly bluish sheen, like moonlight on snow. With her hands she explored her body, seeing it for the first time through new eyes. One hand stroked a slender thigh while the other cupped a firm breast. She closed her eyes and without a trace of shame she stood before them, caressing herself and sighing blissfully at each new sensation.

Pretorius clasped his hands, beaming with pride. 'A glorious abomination.'

Bewildered, Frankenstein could only stare as the naked girl sank to her knees on the floor, the better to reach her hand deep between her legs. He had never encountered such audacious behaviour in a woman before. Not without his calculated seduction, that was. He wasn't sure whether her independence was appealing or threatening. Either way he felt obscurely intimidated.

'Is this your doing?' he asked hoarsely.

'No, my dear Frankenstein. You gave her life. I merely – shall we say, poisoned the waters.'

Justine raised her head in response to their voices and rose slowly to her feet. A smile crept across her features and her predatory gaze softened as her eyes fixed on her creator.

'Frankenstein,' she said plainly.

He eyed her warily as she approached, her arms spread wide, inviting him. Her bosom rose and fell tantalisingly with each breath.

'She has no memory of who she was,' said Pretorius,

'but she seems eager enough to learn the pleasures of the flesh. You must teach her.' He took Justine's hand and presented it to Frankenstein as though joining them in marriage. 'Your master,' he said.

She looked from one man to the other, her mouth twitching in a strange half-smile. There was a touch of madness in it that Frankenstein found disquieting, but he couldn't deny the way his own body was responding to the sight of hers.

'Master,' she said. She slipped her hand free of his and pressed her cool palm against the bulge in his trousers.

With a triumphant laugh Pretorius swept up his cloak and swirled it about his shoulders, fastening it with a jewelled clasp. 'I shall leave you now,' he said, 'to get acquainted.'

For a moment Frankenstein wanted to call him back, but Justine's insistent pressure against his crotch soon banished his uncertainty. She was a newly made creature. And like Pretorius's beloved Cleo, Justine had been released from all sense of human shame or inhibition. Wasn't that what he had wanted after all? A woman free from the restraints of prudish society? Here she stood, naked and willing and gazing hungrily at him as her fingers deftly unfastened his trousers.

He wasted no more time. Hurriedly he unbuttoned his shirt and kicked off his shoes. For a moment he regarded the jars and beakers and retorts on the long wooden table

and then he swept them aside with his arm. He wouldn't
be needing such arcane tools any more. There was the
clink of metal and glass and then the crash of at least
one bottle as it hit the stone floor of the laboratory but
he didn't care. He had recovered from the shock and now
he was drunk on the feeling of power. He had *made* her.

He lifted Justine up onto the table, her slight body
practically weightless in his arms. Her eyes met his and
he lost himself in their piercing blue depths. She was
mesmerising, this alien creature. *His* creature. She lay
still, watching him, her hair spread out beneath her like
a spill of ink, her eyes shining with unnatural desire.

'Take me,' she whispered, her voice a preternatural
growl. 'Fuck me.'

He ran his hands over her, admiring every inch of her
newly awakened flesh. The chill had faded, leaving her
skin feverishly warm beneath his touch. Her nipples were
already hard and he knew what he would find when
he slid his hand lower, to where she had been touching
herself. Sure enough, she was copiously wet.

He hesitated only a moment before shedding the rest
of his clothes and lowering his body onto hers, crushing
her to him. He felt her breasts pressing against his chest
and then her slender legs closed around his own, forcing
his cock towards her sex. Demanding. Insisting.

Immediately he seized her wrists and pinned her hands
down roughly on either side of her. He heard the bones

of her wrists knock against the wood of the table but if it hurt her she gave no sign. Could she even feel pain? He would have to find out, test her responses to a variety of different stimuli, investigate every curve and angle of her reanimated body. There were so many tests to perform and he would thoroughly enjoy every one of them. But there was time enough for that. Right now it was the libertine, not the scientist, who was in command.

'No,' he told her firmly, reasserting his control. 'I'm your master and we'll do things my way.' It was a moment he'd been anticipating for months and he wasn't about to let her direct the proceedings. He searched her face for signs of recognition, of understanding. 'Who am I?' he asked at last.

Again she offered him that catlike half-smile. 'Master,' she said, and it was clear that she understood. Her body language changed completely, became deferential as she lowered her eyes, batting her long lashes demurely. Gone was the wanton slut insisting that he fuck her and in her place was his meek and obedient chambermaid. Or at least the appearance of her.

'Good girl,' he said, releasing her hands so he could stroke her face. 'This is how I like you. Soft and submissive. Do you understand?'

She moaned softly at his touch, turning her head to the side and biting her lip. 'Yes, sir,' she whispered.

Satisfied that he had re-established his authority,

Frankenstein positioned himself at the warm wet entrance to her sex, preparing to take her at last. She gasped as he pressed the head of his cock against her and then she threw back her head with a wild cry as he slid his full length deep inside her. She was tight. Deliciously tight as only a virtuous girl could be. It was a delicacy he so rarely got to enjoy and Justine had certainly been worth the wait.

He thrust into her again and again and her hips rose eagerly to meet him each time. Bottles clinked against one another as the force of his thrusts rocked the table. There was the occasional crash as one toppled to the floor, followed by the pungent smell of some chemical released into the air. Outside the storm continued to rage. Lightning illuminated the room, painting Justine's skin an even more otherworldly blue that he found perversely beautiful.

He met her eyes and was once more transported by their depth, by the hint within them of the secret things they had seen, of the forbidden knowledge they possessed. Then she arched back on the table and he ran a finger up the line of her breastbone. She moaned with pleasure and her breath caught as he lowered his mouth to her ripe nipples, devouring her with his lips and tongue, while he continued to fuck her.

Justine eased her legs around him, gently letting them encircle his waist. At one point she met his eyes with a meek and silent question and he felt himself grow even harder at her subservience. He rewarded her with an approving smile and she closed her eyes in bliss as she squeezed him between her surprisingly powerful thighs.

She was astonishing, a creature of singular beauty and mystery. And all the while he fucked her, he reminded himself that she was his. His creation, his plaything. She belonged to him and to no other. The feeling of omnipotence, of mastery over her, was almost as intoxicating as her physical allure.

He slowed his strokes and forced himself to savour the moment. She watched him with curiosity and then dismay as he stopped and eased himself out.

'Don't worry. We're not finished, my little pet.'

He pulled her to her feet and admired her nakedness for a moment before turning her around to face the table. Then he directed her forwards so that she was bending over it. He positioned her how he wanted her: forearms on the table, head up, back arched, bottom out. He didn't intend to bugger her just yet. That particular pleasure could wait until he'd broken her in a bit more. But he wanted to have her from behind, to admire the curve of her supple spine, her long slender neck, her wild dark hair.

'Good girl,' he said, and she dipped her head with feline grace.

He took a moment to stroke the velvety softness of her bottom, gently running his fingers over the rounded curve of each cheek before tracing the line between them and finding her dewy slit again.

Justine moaned and squirmed at his touch, begging him with her body to fuck her again. She rose on her toes and wiggled her bottom from side to side. He sensed it was all she could do to keep from voicing her desperation.

He didn't torment her – or himself – for long. He spread the soft folds of her sex and guided his cock in again, pushing himself in and out with long, slow, languid strokes. Justine threw her head back with each thrust and he took hold of her hair, winding it around his hand and pulling it tight. With his other hand he reached around to her breasts, squeezing and pinching her tender nipples and delighting in the little cries his actions elicited.

When her legs began to quake with the strain of the position he'd put her in, he released her and turned her around again. He wanted to see her face as she came. And it didn't take long at all before a spectacular climax tore through her. She opened her mouth wide in a silent scream, her eyes shut tight as she succumbed to the sensations. Her sex clenched and contracted around him, pulsing with a hot fury he'd never have dreamt her capable of. The spasms of her body brought about his own orgasm and the sheer force of it made him dizzy. The world went black behind his eyes and for many moments nothing existed but ecstasy.

When he was at last able to get up he looked down at his deflowered maid. A smear of blood stood out in stark relief on her pale splayed thighs. Tenderly he wiped it away with a cloth. Justine lay still as he did, watching him with those strange, unfathomable eyes.

Now that his lust was sated, he could examine the more intellectual aspects of the experiment. Was the girl truly defined by her sexual instincts, as Pretorius had suggested? Or was there more going on beneath the surface? He got dressed as he turned various thoughts over in his mind.

Certainly he must keep her under lock and key. He couldn't take the chance of anyone recognising her. Justine the chambermaid had perished in the river and her kind employer had seen to the funeral arrangements. He might have sent her home to her family for all anyone knew. She could quietly resume her duties within his house but he would have to answer the door himself from now on lest anyone catch sight of her. Oh, but that would be such a bore. He looked at her, frowning.

She mirrored his expression as though trying it on for herself. She hadn't moved from where she lay.

All at once he had the solution. 'Of course! You weren't dead after all.'

She peered at him quizzically.

'Yes,' he continued, more to himself than to her. 'The frozen river. The icy water. You simply weren't dead. How

would a pair of ignorant dockworkers know anyway?'
He nodded emphatically, pleased with himself. He still
had no intention of letting her out of his sight, but now
he had an explanation that would satisfy even the most
determined busybody.

Justine's brow furrowed as she listened to him. She
looked somewhat pensive, but she seemed to understand
what he was saying. Her mind appeared as unscathed
as her body. Truly, she had lost nothing but her identity.
And her virginity, of course.

'I saved you,' he said decisively. 'It's as simple as
that.'

'Saved,' she echoed, drawing out the word. 'Mmmm.
Thank you, sir.'

'You're very welcome,' he said.

A smile tugged at her lips and she ran her hands over
her naked body with a little sigh he took for an invitation to enjoy her further.

'No,' he said, bewildered by her stamina. 'I think
you've had enough excitement for one night. As have I.
And as much as I adore the sight of you naked, I don't
want you to catch a chill.'

Mischievous laughter danced in her eyes at that and
he felt vaguely unnerved. She knew things that he did
not and it disturbed him greatly.

He pushed the feeling aside as he helped her to her feet.
Although she stood naked in the cold stone laboratory,

she didn't seem in danger of catching any chill. And as he led her out of the laboratory and down the stairs to her room he suspected that the cold would never trouble her again.

CHAPTER SIX

A New Life

Sleep fell away from her like coils of soft rope and Justine opened her eyes, shedding the remnants of the most extraordinary dream. Bright, yellow fingers of sunlight lay across the bed, making her think of a giant hand holding her down. For a moment she imagined a woman so small she could fit into a man's palm, but then she laughed at the silly notion. It had all been part of her dream.

She stretched and sat up, surprised by the brightness of the light. Her body felt stiff, as though she'd been asleep for days. It must be late afternoon, meaning she'd missed the entire morning. Startled, she struggled free of the tangled bedclothes and scrambled to dress herself. Dream images adhered to her like cobwebs and she found herself unable to account for the vivid nature of some of it.

She saw herself standing on a bridge, her tears turning

to ice as she contemplated the frozen oblivion below. She could almost feel the cold burn of the water as she plunged into it. The icy currents embraced her and she floated, then sank. Then there was the storm. The thunder, the lightning. And a kind man peeling away layer upon layer of her skin to reveal ... what? Had she been injured? Was she healed now? Glancing down, she satisfied herself that she was quite undamaged.

The plain black uniform she found was familiar to her and her fingers knotted the strings of her pinafore as though they had performed the act dozens of times. But still she was confused. Where was she and what was she meant to be doing? Her body seemed to remember some sort of purpose but her mind was blank. Most alarming of all, she found she did not know who she was. Everything about her surroundings was familiar, but it was like a place visited after an absence of many years. Was it possible she was still dreaming?

A glance out the small window grounded her somewhat and a name came to her at last. Dr Frankenstein. Her master. Yes, she remembered him from last night. Her sex pulsed warmly at the thought of him and she closed her eyes. But the image that came to her then must have been part of her dream. For surely she had never ...

Almost of its own accord her hand strayed down between her legs to stroke the velvety softness through the split in her drawers. There was a peculiar soreness there that wasn't entirely unpleasant. As she pictured her master's kind face she couldn't repress the thought that it was *his* hand caressing her. And then more than his hand. She felt a rush of desire so intense it made her dizzy.

She shook her head and blinked herself out of the fantasy. Heavens! What would any gentleman think of a maid who slept half the day and then abused his kindness in such a shameful way? It was wrong. And yet it was only a distant part of her that seemed to think it was wrong. She couldn't keep the thoughts from her mind and it seemed the most natural thing in the world to indulge them. Her pulse quickened even as she smoothed down her skirt and set about pinning up her long dark hair. The looking-glass teased her with the image of her flushed cheeks and she went to the basin in the corner and splashed her face with water. Once she was satisfied with her appearance she headed downstairs, determined to make apologies for her lateness and to banish any further indecent thoughts.

She hesitated on the landing, wondering how to explain her confusion, or whether she even should. Perhaps everything would come flooding back to her in a rush. She didn't want to trouble her master with such a trivial affliction if she might be fine again in a matter of hours. If only she could –

'Justine! What are you doing out of bed?'

She jumped at the sound of a familiar voice and looked

down to see a man on the stairs. She knew him at once. Knew his face, his voice and the elegant cut of his clothes. Why, then, was her own self still such a mystery to her? Justine? Was that her name?

'Sir, I'm sorry I overslept. I must have –'

'I let you sleep,' he said gently, taking her arm and steering her back up the stairs. 'Don't you remember the accident?'

'Accident?'

'Yes.' He stopped at the door to her room and peered deeply into her eyes, as though searching for something. The touch of his hands and the nearness of him was filling her head with erotic images again and she pressed her legs together. 'Has your memory returned?'

So he knew. She sighed with relief that she neither had to try to explain nor hide anything from him. She shook her head slowly. 'But I'm not dead,' she said decisively.

For a moment he looked startled by her words. She wasn't even sure where they had come from; they'd simply popped into her mind. But then he smiled. 'No, you're not dead. In fact, you're very much alive, my dear girl.' He cupped her face in his hands. 'And who you were before is of no consequence. All that befell you in the end was a slight case of amnesia. And a small mercy, that, given the unhappiness that drove you to the river in the first place.'

The river. Her frozen tears. The icy swirling currents.

So it hadn't been a dream after all. And if that part was real, then the rest of it must have been real too. Another wave of desire came over her and her skin prickled beneath her starchy clothes. She felt constricted by all of it: the chemise, the drawers, the pins pulling her hair away from her face.

'Are you in pain?' Frankenstein asked, seeing her discomfort.

She tugged at the collar of her uniform. 'It's just so hot.'

He looked surprised. 'None of the fires are lit. The house is freezing.'

'I can keep you warm.' The words had left her mouth before she'd had a chance to consider them. But she liked the way saying them made her feel almost as much as she liked his startled expression. She wanted to be naked. She wanted him. And before he could speak she was halfway through unbuttoning her dress.

But he stopped her.

'No,' he said, taking her firmly by the wrist. 'We have work to do today, my girl. And as you're already awake we might as well start. Pretorius is waiting.'

She opened her mouth to repeat the strange name, but Frankenstein was already leading her up the stairs. He took her to a room at the top of the house and she blinked at her surroundings. She knew this place. This was where she'd been last night.

'My dear girl!'

Justine looked up in surprise as another man – Pretorius, she guessed – came towards her. He wore a lavish wine-red coat and his face beamed with joy as he saw her. He seemed vaguely familiar and for a moment she faltered, wondering if he was someone she ought to know. He had been here for a short while the night before, hadn't he? Yes, he'd helped her in some way. She searched his face for answers to her silent queries but he turned to Frankenstein instead. Then he said something that made no sense to her at all.

'We've done well, my dear boy.'

Frankenstein frowned slightly and shook his head, puzzling Justine even further by his reaction.

'Saving her life, I mean,' Pretorius said with a laugh.

Frankenstein seemed to relax. 'Yes, of course.'

'I trust you enjoyed yourself after I left?'

Now Justine remembered him. He had introduced her to Frankenstein and said he was her master. She remembered him taking her arm, guiding her across the floor, unwinding the bandages from her limbs. She remembered the skylight and the flashes of lightning. And the table … Ah, yes, she remembered that most of all. Her heart began to pound and she sighed as she thought of his hands caressing her warm naked flesh in the cold room.

Frankenstein followed her gaze to the disordered table and for a moment he looked uneasy. Then she recalled something he'd said to her. That he liked her soft and submissive. Immediately she adopted a more modest demeanour, lowering her head and peering up at him.

He nodded his approval and led her to a strange device in the corner of the room. She supposed it was another sort of table, but the metal cranks, straps and pulleys made her think of something from a mediaeval dungeon.

From somewhere behind her she heard Pretorius laugh.

'The poor girl thinks we're about to torture her! Ah, but perhaps she'd enjoy that too?' He took her chin between his thumb and forefinger and gave her a lascivious wink. 'My Cleo is certainly no stranger to a little pain.'

Cleo. The name seemed to ring the very faintest of bells. But the more Justine tried to fix it in her mind the more it eluded her. It was probably just another detail from her strange dream.

Frankenstein took Justine by the arm and pulled her away, shooting Pretorius a look. 'Careful,' he said.

Then without another word he began to undress her. She stood still, her body tingling with anticipation. She longed for him to touch her in her most sensitive places, but he seemed to be studiously avoiding those. When she finally stood naked before him he looked her up and down, but there was none of the unbridled lust she'd seen the night before. Indeed, his eyes still gleamed with fascination, but it was of a more detached and clinical kind.

Her desires must have been written on her face, for

Pretorius arched an eyebrow at Frankenstein. 'Exquisite,' he said. 'And so deliciously eager.'

'Yes,' Frankenstein agreed. 'Perhaps a little *too* eager.'

He helped her up onto the strange device and positioned her so that she was lying on her back. She angled her legs apart, a meek and silent request which he pointedly ignored.

'Now then,' he said, 'I want to see how you respond to various stimuli. But I'm going to have to restrain you so you don't injure yourself.'

With that he buckled her wrists into a pair of leather straps, cinching them tight. These he fastened to a bar behind her head so that she was stretched to her full length. The position forced her back into an arch, thrusting her breasts up. She sighed with pleasure at the feeling of helpless exposure. Next he gave her ankles the same treatment, pulling her body taut with the turn of a crank. Justine tugged at the restraints and confirmed that she was held fast. The knowledge sent a hot pulse through her sex and she writhed a little to show him the effect it was having on her.

But if he noticed he gave no sign. He stood over her and his eyes travelled the length of her bare flesh as though she were merely a laboratory specimen to be experimented upon. She wondered whether Pretorius could see what she wanted, and whether he might convey her needs to his friend. Or possibly even see to her himself.

At last Frankenstein touched her, but it was the touch of a clinician, not a lover. He ran his fingers lightly over her thigh and she shivered.

'She certainly feels that,' Pretorius said from somewhere behind her. The idea that he was watching the proceedings only added to her sense of arousal.

'What about this?' Frankenstein asked.

The fingers moved higher, circling her abdomen.

She moaned at his nearness to her sex. 'Yes,' she whispered.

Now the fingers of both hands crept up along the sides of her ribcage, coming tantalisingly close to her breasts. 'This?'

Justine's breathing grew fast and shallow as she willed him to touch her properly, to kiss her, to fuck her as he had the night before. To have her again and again. The thought of being taken while she was bound and helpless was painfully erotic and she closed her eyes, remembering the feel of his cock inside her.

A scratching noise distracted her from her reverie and she glanced up to see that he had moved away and was writing in a leather-bound book. His face was set in deep concentration, as though it were vitally important that he record her every response. She hoped he was making notes on the responses that were of most importance to *her*.

Suddenly Pretorius was beside her. He had an object in his hand and it took her a moment to work out that it was a fountain pen. A smile was playing on his lips. He pressed the sharp nib of the pen against her belly and began very slowly and carefully to write. She shuddered at the ticklish sensation, straining helplessly in her bonds as he dipped the nib into a pot of ink and continued writing.

'What are you doing?' Frankenstein asked.

'Just reminding myself of the formula,' Pretorius said with a small laugh. 'I think perhaps I may need to dilute it in future.'

Justine had no idea what he was talking about, but she enjoyed the sensation of the pen inscribing her flesh. She pictured herself completely covered in ink, clothed only in writing. Cryptic symbols to her but words that would have special meaning for the two men. They could take turns reading her, then wiping the words away so they might start again. Her mind went wild with the endless possibilities.

Frankenstein made another note in his journal and then returned to her side. His eyes travelled the length of her stretched body and he raised one hand to stroke her foot. Excitement flared in her like lightning. He methodically pinched her toes one by one, then cupped her foot in his hand and tested its sensitivity in various tender places.

Pretorius had stopped writing to watch, fascinated.

'Extraordinary,' Frankenstein said, transferring his attention to her other foot and eliciting the same response. 'It's as though every inch of flesh has become an erogenous zone.'

He stared down at her for several seconds before at last placing his hand on her breast. She arched into his touch as he squeezed her gently. Then his thumb slid lazily over her nipple, making her gasp. Justine thought she would explode.

He shook his head in astonishment. 'I've never seen such sustained arousal in my life.'

'I have,' Pretorius said, beaming proudly.

'Yes, well, I'm not sure it's entirely healthy.'

Justine whimpered softly as her master's fingers closed around both her nipples, gently at first and then gradually exerting more pressure until he was pinching her quite hard. She closed her eyes, hissing through her teeth as she allowed the sensation to wash over her. It hurt, but it was a pain that shaded into pleasure. When he let go he watched her face, observing her reaction rather than asking her if she'd felt it.

Whatever he read in her face must have given him an idea because he went to a cupboard in the corner of the room and there was a clattering as he fished around in a drawer.

'I think,' he said to Pretorius, 'this might make things more interesting.'

He held up a short length of black cloth and without a word he wrapped it around Justine's eyes and tied it behind her head.

'Can you see anything?' he asked her.

She blinked behind the blindfold, trying to peer through the material, but all she could see were murky dark shapes. She shook her head.

'Good.'

Deprived of her sight, she became more aware of her other senses. She heard the clink of something small and metal and then the scrape of a shoe on the stone floor as Frankenstein bent over her. He pinched her right nipple and then there was the sensation of something much harder than his fingers closing around it like teeth. For a moment she thought he had bitten her but then he drew away and the feeling began to intensify. And just as when he had pinched her before, it grew from something like pain into almost unbearable pleasure.

The pressure increased even more and she realised he had fastened something on to her nipple, something hard and metal. She whimpered as he tightened it further and the pain began to seethe and flow through her like sweet poison. The murmur of voices reached her through the haze. She had no idea what they were saying.

The delicious pain hadn't yet reached its peak when she felt him take hold of her other nipple and she braced herself for the same treatment. With a sharp intake of breath she held still as he positioned the metal clamp, tightening it gradually. Exquisite sensations blossomed within her and she writhed in her bonds, moaning and whimpering by turns.

She had the sense of a charged stillness all around her and she imagined the two men watching her intently, studying her and gauging her responses. Although her ankles were secured, she was still able to angle her legs apart by opening her knees, offering herself for further experimentation.

The low hum of their voices followed and then her master's hands were spreading the lips of her sex. She gritted her teeth, bracing herself. Tiny metal jaws closed gently, first on one side, then the other, and her body was alive with pleasure and pain. The two had become indistinguishable.

After a little while there came a harder sound, a solid clank as something new was produced. She held her breath as she waited to see where it would go, what it would do and how it would feel. A warm finger stroked the opening of her sex and she heard her master's voice like distant music. He told her to be still and she obeyed. Then the device entered her.

It was harder than his cock had been and it filled her completely. Instantly her muscles contracted around it, welcoming it. She moved her hips to encourage it deeper and Frankenstein obliged her. Then he placed his hand on her abdomen and pressed down firmly, touching the metal object through the thin wall of skin. It was a strange, vaguely uncomfortable sensation that made all the tiny hairs on her body stand on end. And yet at the same time its very discomfort was somehow pleasant as well.

He moved the metal shaft inside her, drawing it slowly in and out as though he were fucking her, all the while exerting pressure from outside with his hand. She had the feeling of being laid completely bare, all her insides on display for his use and pleasure. Each time he pushed the object back inside her he brushed against the clamps. Vibrations chimed through her.

She felt a climax building within her and for a moment she feared she wouldn't be able to take it, that the pleasure would overwhelm her. Tears filled her eyes, dampening the blindfold, but her body only wanted more.

Then her master spoke to her. 'Not yet,' he said clearly, right in her ear. 'You are not to let go until I give you permission. Do you understand?'

A hot flush of excitement spread over her face and throat and she managed to nod her head.

He repeated the question.

'Yes, sir,' she whispered, fighting to keep herself back from the edge. She didn't know if she could stop herself, but she hated the thought of disappointing him.

'Shall we turn her over?' Pretorius asked.

'Certainly,' Frankenstein said. 'I'm eager to see how she responds to this.' There was another metallic clank and Justine shuddered with delirious anticipation. 'But first I think we had better remove these.'

The pressure against her nipples was renewed. The clamps opened and the blood flow returned with a sudden rush of agony so intense it made her cry out. Her nipples burned and throbbed, but the pain quickly faded to a pleasant tingling that only made her want more. Her nether lips suffered the same as the clamps were removed but the device inside her sex was left in place.

She heard Pretorius give a delighted laugh. 'It's as though her body perceives pain as pleasure. Her senses don't interpret it the way ours do.'

'Yes. It's an interesting ... side effect.'

Before she had a chance to wonder what they meant, she heard the turning of a crank and she felt herself rotating with the table. They made some adjustment to her arms and legs and then they turned her onto her front, leaving her hands and feet bound. Justine felt defenceless and utterly at their mercy. She was an empty vessel awaiting whatever her master chose to fill her with. They could do anything they wanted to her and she would have no choice but to take it. To submit, to absorb, to suffer. The knowledge was both frightening and exhilarating.

A hand stroked her bottom and she smiled to herself as she recognised her master's touch. His hands were softer than his friend's. She felt his fingers tracing her delicate curves and she shivered as his thumbs crept further in and gently parted her cheeks. Then he slid a finger up the cleft of her bottom and she flinched.

'Relax,' Frankenstein said.

She did as he said and immediately his fingertip touched her bottom-hole. There was a slippery sensation as he daubed her with something and then his finger was demanding entry, pushing firmly up inside her. She gasped with pleasure as he drew his finger in and out, swirling it round inside her and spreading her open. Then he withdrew it and she lay panting for a moment before he pressed a hard smooth object against the opening. Another metal rod like the one already filling her sex. It slipped inside her easily and the sensation of being penetrated in both places at once was an ecstasy almost past enduring.

The two rods rubbed against each other on either side of the delicate veil that separated them inside her and she bit down on her outstretched arm, muffling a cry against her skin. The rods moved in opposition, as though she were being fucked by two men at once. But two men made of cold steel. Unyielding and inescapable. It was too much. She knew she would never be able to control herself. And just before she was forced to shame herself by letting go, her master instructed her to come.

With a wild cry she clenched herself around both metal shafts, embracing them as she abandoned herself to the chaos of a pounding orgasm that sent shock waves through every nerve in her body, devastating her.

She had no idea how long she lay there afterwards before they finally untied her, but the tone of their voices seemed to indicate that they were pleased with her performance. There was more scratching as notes were made and observations were recorded. When they released her at last, her master stroked her hair and told her she had done very well. Then he removed the blindfold and helped her to her feet. Her legs were unsteady and she leant on him until they had stopped trembling. He wrapped a blanket around her and guided her to a chair and sat her down.

Frankenstein and Pretorius conferred while Justine recovered her senses, but it wasn't long before her body began to want more. The tingling grew ever more intense and she tried to sit still as she'd been told. But it was impossible. She shrugged off the blanket and slid down in the chair, spreading her legs wide as her hands gently stroked her throbbing sex.

The men turned to watch her, wide-eyed with amazement.

CHAPTER SEVEN

Friend

Daisy stood nervously on the doorstep, shivering from more than just the cold. She was trying to gather the courage to ring the bell. Twice before, she had come to the house but lost her nerve, scampering back to her father's bookshop like a stray dog chased away from scraps. Granted, that had been for an entirely other purpose, but she was still intimidated by the prospect of seeing Dr Frankenstein again. Ever since the anatomy lesson she had been hoping he would contact her, to offer her another chance to do her part for medical science. There was certainly no way she could afford his professional services. But alas, it seemed that her one experience with him was to be her last.

Oh, but she shouldn't even be thinking such things when she was here on such mournful business as this!

'Wicked girl,' she hissed, giving her arm a vicious

pinch. If only she'd been able to afford roses instead of
the sad little bunch of violets and pinks, she might press
the thorns to her skin as proper penance for her sins.

Tears sprang to her eyes as she thought of Justine.
Poor Justine who had given her heart away only to have
it trodden in the mud. How she missed her friend. She
hadn't even had a chance to say goodbye. All she could
hope was that Dr Frankenstein would give her that chance
now. Summoning her wits, she rang the bell and waited.

She never heard the approach of footsteps, so when the
door suddenly rattled open it made her jump. She gave
a little cry as she dropped the flowers and immediately
ducked down to retrieve them from the snow at her feet.

'I'm most awfully sorry, sir,' she babbled, gathering the
flowers into an even sorrier bunch than they had been in
when she arrived. 'I just came to pay my ...' She froze.
The final word fell like a stone into a well. 'Respects.'

'Do I know you?' Justine asked.

Daisy stared in open-mouthed wonder at what could
only be a ghost. Her friend stood before her, dressed in
her black dress and white pinafore, just as Daisy had
always seen her. Just as if nothing had happened. Her
mind whirled and it was only after a considerable silence
that she was finally able to speak again. 'Justine?'

The girl frowned slightly. 'You know me,' she said,
'yet I don't know you.'

'It's me. Daisy.'

Justine repeated the name as though tasting a sweet. 'Daisy. Yes, I like that name.' She smiled. But it wasn't the smile of the demure Justine that Daisy knew. There was something strange about it. Something knowing. Justine's eyes glinted like stolen jewels.

Feeling uneasy, Daisy glanced down at the flowers she was holding. Her clutching hand had broken most of the stems. Not that it mattered now. She tossed them aside and forced herself to meet her friend's eyes. 'Don't you remember me?'

'There was an accident,' Justine said matter-of-factly.

Daisy remembered the men who had come to her that night, bearing the cold wet body of her friend. They'd allowed Daisy a tiny glimpse of Justine's pale, serene face before covering her up again. Her eyes streaming with tears, Daisy had told them where Justine lived and they had promised to see that she was delivered into safe hands.

'But you drowned,' Daisy said in an awed whisper. She couldn't bring herself to add that she'd seen her body.

'I was saved,' Justine said, smiling. 'My master saved me.'

At last the reality sank in and Daisy broke into a relieved smile of her own. Saved. Of course! Frankenstein was a doctor, after all. Justine must have only been unconscious when she was pulled from the river. Overwhelmed by the sudden joy, Daisy threw her arms around Justine and kissed her cheek. 'You're alive!' she cried.

Rose de Fer

Justine's arms encircled Daisy after a moment and she returned the embrace. Then she turned Daisy's face to hers and kissed her full on the mouth.

Daisy gave a small squeak of surprise beneath the kiss, but she only struggled for a moment. Her heart leapt at the contact and all at once the passion she had felt throughout Frankenstein's demonstration was reawakened. She'd read about such passion between women, but never supposed those stories to be true, never supposed that another girl would feel that way towards her. Now that her friend was pushing her tongue deep into her mouth, however, she surrendered to her own surge of longing. Justine was beautiful. And her ordeal seemed to have only made her more so. Her skin was so soft, so silky, her mouth so warm and inviting. Daisy wanted to lose herself in the kiss, to drown in it and never resurface.

Boldly she slipped her hand between their bodies and pressed it against the gentle swell of her friend's bosom. Justine's kiss grew fiercer at Daisy's touch and she reciprocated, her slender fingers tracing the outline of Daisy's rather fuller breasts beneath her dress and heavy coat.

Daisy felt herself growing damp and even as she registered the thought Justine's hand crept down to stroke her through her skirt. She gasped at the teasing contact, desperately wishing she could yank up Justine's skirt and caress the swollen wetness she knew she would find there. Caress it and kiss it.

90

'Justine!'

The girls broke apart at the sound of the male voice. Red-faced, Daisy dropped her eyes to her shabby boots but Justine faced their accuser as though they'd done nothing wrong.

'Yes, sir?'

Frankenstein stood glowering in the doorway for a moment before seizing Daisy by the arm and yanking her inside. He slammed the door and Daisy cowered by the umbrella stand. Justine merely looked puzzled.

'What in God's name do you think you're doing?'

His question seemed to be addressed to both of them and Daisy immediately babbled another apology. He waved it away.

'Anyone might pass by and see you,' he told Justine. 'And you –' here he rounded on Daisy '– what are you doing here?'

Tears leaked from her eyes and her words came out in a rush. 'Sir, I only wanted to ask you if I might say goodbye to Justine but then she answered the door and I saw she was unharmed after all. I'm sorry, sir. I was just so relieved and I suppose I was quite overcome.'

He raised an eyebrow and offered her a sardonic smile. 'I had noticed. Well, my girl, don't you think it's rather a tawdry way to show your appreciation?'

'Sir! I was only ...' She glanced at Justine, who was watching the exchange impassively. She wouldn't tell him it had been Justine who had initiated things. 'I meant no harm.'

Frankenstein ran a hand through his hair and looked from one girl to the other in exasperation. Daisy had no idea what he was thinking or why he appeared to be so disturbed. She hadn't got the impression that he was a man easily shocked. After all, if even a simple bookseller's daughter knew about such things, surely an educated man like him did. And likely more besides.

Then his expression softened. He took Daisy by the arm and led her off to one side. 'Listen,' he said gently, 'Justine has had a terrible experience and she hasn't fully recovered from it yet. She lost her memory in the accident and she's still in a very delicate state.'

Daisy's heart sank. 'Lost her memory?'

He nodded. 'She doesn't even remember her name. Or you.'

If he meant to imply that Justine was not in control of her actions, that her passion moments before had been merely a sign of her disordered mind, well, Daisy wasn't convinced. Behind his back Justine smiled and licked her lips, as though still tasting Daisy.

'I had hoped to keep her away from outside influences until her memory returned, but I fear it may never come back.'

Something about the whole situation seemed wrong to Daisy and she frowned. 'But, sir, surely outside influences are just what she needs to bring her back. To remind her.'

His eyes flashed at her boldness, but there was a trace of worry in them too. Daisy knew that look well. It was the look of a man trying to hide something. Clearly he didn't want anyone to see Justine but she didn't think it was because he was so concerned for her wellbeing. There was something else going on here.

'I understand, sir,' she said, choosing her words carefully. 'You don't want to upset her. Well, you can rely on me, sir. I shan't let anyone know what's happened.'

The look of anxiety left his face and he patted her shoulder. 'I knew you'd understand, Daisy. You're a good girl.'

She smiled sweetly and held his eyes long enough to let him know that *she* knew something was afoot. He registered the look and Daisy turned back to Justine, who was still watching silently, a cryptic look of her own on her face.

Daisy gave her a sisterly hug and whispered in her ear, 'Send me word when it's safe to come back.'

Justine returned the hug tightly, crushing her breasts against Daisy's and sighing with contentment. 'Come tonight. I'll leave the back door unlocked.'

Daisy's heart leapt but she kept her expression neutral as she pulled away. 'I hope you feel better soon,' she said for Frankenstein's benefit.

He let Daisy out without a word and she couldn't keep the smile from her face as she made her way back to the bookshop, where she counted the minutes until nightfall.

* * *

'Are you sure he's asleep?'

Justine smiled. 'He never sleeps. He's in his laboratory working. Come on.'

Daisy followed her up the back stairs and into a room on the second floor. It was surprisingly large for a servant's room, but then Justine had always said that Frankenstein was a generous master. A small fire burned in the grate and shadows danced across the walls.

'I thought you might be cold,' Justine said, easing Daisy out of her coat.

'Aren't *you*?'

Justine shook her head. Smiling, she removed Daisy's gloves one at a time. Then her bonnet.

That morning Daisy could easily have lost herself in their moment of indiscretion, but now that she was here for a proper lovers' assignation she suddenly felt shy and uncertain. 'Justine, I … I'm not sure we …'

But Justine appeared to have no inhibitions. She slipped out of her dress and Daisy gasped to see that she wore nothing underneath. Daisy had never seen another girl naked before. She had only seen drawings in her father's forbidden books. Now, confronted with the real thing, she couldn't take her eyes off Justine.

'You're beautiful,' she said, her voice a breathless whisper. She smiled to see that Justine's sex was bare like her own. Frankenstein had shaved her before the anatomy lesson and Daisy had enjoyed the sensation so much that she had kept it up herself. Of course, she had been hoping that Frankenstein would be the one to see it, that he would introduce her to the strange contraption he'd described at the lecture.

She'd fantasised often about the whole experience, embellishing it with little touches that made it more exciting for her, and she'd longed to tell Justine about it. But the Justine she had known back then had been so innocent that Daisy hadn't wanted to shock her. Now it didn't seem to matter. Justine had apparently found her own desires.

Daisy swallowed as she continued to gaze at the naked female body before her. It was a thing of wonder, all soft curves and smooth lines. So unlike the harsh angles of the male physique. She realised that, in all the time she'd been sneaking peeks at Oriental drawings, she had never paid much attention to the men in the pictures. It was only the women who captured her interest. And sometimes late at night she would close her eyes and allow her hand to slip inside her nightgown and imagine herself in a harem, surrounded only by her own fair sex …

Rose de Fer

'Now you,' Justine said, her eyes sparkling.

Daisy blushed and glanced down at herself, at her drab blue dress, her worn stockings. She couldn't help but think that her body beneath would be just as dull. 'Oh, I don't know,' she began, but Justine was already reaching for her.

'Don't be silly,' Justine said. Her fingers quickly unfastened the buttons of Daisy's dress.

As first the patched jacket and then the skirt came away, Daisy closed her eyes. Justine didn't hesitate when she reached Daisy's underclothes; she unlaced the drawers and slipped them down before pulling the chemise off over Daisy's head. Instinctively, Daisy's hands flew to cover her breasts, but Justine eased them away.

'I want to see you,' Justine said, stepping back for a better look.

Although she was warm enough before the fire, Daisy couldn't suppress her trembling. It was impossible to believe that she was being seduced by her dearest friend. Justine seemed so different, so changed. She was so eerily confident. Daisy wanted her to take control, to tell her what to do. Anything Justine asked of her, she would do.

'Lovely,' Justine said. She wrapped her arms around Daisy and pulled her in for a deep kiss. Daisy's body responded at once and she relaxed into the moment, welcoming Justine's probing tongue into her mouth and reciprocating. Daisy's hands travelled up and down the

96

length of her friend's body before finally fitting themselves over her breasts. They were so much smaller than her own. Barely a handful. Justine's body was shorter and slighter and yet Daisy felt by far the more vulnerable.

Justine pulled away and let her fingers trail over Daisy's breasts. Instantly her nipples hardened at the attention and Daisy held her breath as Justine dipped her head and kissed each stiff little peak. With the tip of her tongue she drew lazy circles around each one, while her hand traced its way down Daisy's front, down to where she was slick with the juices of her excitement. Daisy was aching for more, but she was mesmerised by the stillness of the moment.

When Justine's fingers reached the dewy folds of her sex Daisy bit back a little cry. She was terrified that they would be interrupted, that something would break the spell, that Justine would suddenly snap out of it and tell Daisy she was a filthy girl. But none of that happened. Instead Justine began sliding her finger back and forth across the engorged bud of Daisy's clitoris. With a gasp Daisy clamped her legs around Justine's hand, afraid her legs would buckle.

Justine cocked her head, giving her a lopsided smile, as though she found Daisy's reaction curious and amusing. Daisy immediately slipped her own hand between Justine's legs and Justine moaned softly in response. She opened her legs so Daisy could caress her. Her inner thighs were slick with moisture and the thought that Justine was so aroused filled her with even more passion. Daisy dipped a finger inside her.

With a soft cry Justine arched her back, exposing her throat for Daisy to kiss. Daisy could feel Justine's pulse beneath her tongue and she had the mad thought that she was tasting life itself. The tiny throb was so strong, so vibrant. She couldn't help but think how she'd almost lost Justine and it filled her with a sense of urgency. She backed Justine towards the bed and they tumbled into it.

Daisy kissed her way down every inch of Justine's luminous body, biting softly at the tender skin of her inner thighs before daring to go further. Justine spread her legs wide, inviting Daisy to kiss her where her fingers had already been. Her sleek wetness gleamed in the firelight, the shadows playing over the hills and valleys of her mound and open legs. Justine bent her knees and angled her pelvis up like an offering and Daisy lowered her head to the warm wet centre, inhaling the rich musky scent of her arousal. She had never dared to imagine such a moment and even when she pressed her lips to the swollen bud of Justine's clitoris she could hardly believe it was happening.

Justine gave a soft cry and there was a creak as she gripped the iron bars of the headboard. Her body tensed and contracted, quivering with desire. Daisy swirled her tongue slowly round the little nub, flicking it back and forth as she had with her fingers, making Justine gasp. With her hands she kneaded the slender thighs on either side, pushing her tongue deep inside as she did so.

Daisy allowed her tender strokes to grow more and more frenzied and Justine's hips rocked back and forth as Daisy kissed her, licking, sucking, devouring her. At last the pleasure overtook her and Justine stiffened and shuddered violently. Daisy pressed her tongue against the slick crease and sighed as she felt each little throb. Hysterical paroxysm. Wasn't that what Dr Frankenstein had called it?

Since then Daisy had learnt that one didn't need a physician to achieve it, but she still couldn't help imagining the powerful device he had described during the lecture. So large it couldn't be transported, he'd said. The elaborate fantasy she had entertained during the demonstration had often obsessed her but she had found herself focusing less on the dispassionate doctor and more on his cowled lady assistant. Only now did she realise who it was beneath the cowl. Who it had always been.

She raised her head to find Justine watching her, a cryptic smile playing on her face. Daisy flushed and looked away as though she'd been caught doing something she shouldn't.

'I can show you things,' Justine said dreamily, 'that will make you fly.'

And before the night was over she had taken Daisy downstairs to Frankenstein's rooms and introduced her to the machine she had dreamt of for so long.

CHAPTER EIGHT

Frustration

Frankenstein frowned at the note. Mrs Sylvia Leigh-Hunt was frightfully sorry but she had pressing matters to deal with and wouldn't be able to see him for a while. He'd received a similar note from his newest conquest, a wide-eyed American heiress named Lillian Wingate, whose impotent husband had sent her to him honestly believing the climate to be the cause of her distemper. But now she too was apparently beset by more pressing matters. What could possibly be more pressing than their repressed sexual needs? He crumpled both notes in his fist and hurled them into the fire where they blackened and burned, quickly turning to ash.

And where was Justine? Ever since that wretched Daisy had sniffed her out she'd scarcely been around to carry out her duties. Instead she smiled sweetly at him and told him how lovely it was to stroll through the park in the snow. Alone. Ah, but one couldn't deceive a deceiver. He knew love – or at least lust – was in the air; he could smell its cloying scent. He'd turned a blind eye to their dalliance the night she'd sneaked Daisy in but things were getting out of hand. Now she blatantly defied him. She disobeyed his instructions to stay inside the house and there was no telling what she and Daisy got up to together.

Not that he especially cared. As exciting as the concept had seemed at first, a sexually liberated woman was more a curse than a blessing. Daisy was probably doing him a favour by giving Justine an outlet. How could he ever have guessed that the thrill of the chase would turn out to be the best part? That a hard-fought battle was more fun than the actual victory? His unique abilities simply weren't required with a woman who was always hungry and demanding. And although he'd instructed Justine to be submissive, he knew it was an act. Behind those haunting eyes she was merely humouring him. Or worse: pitying him. In either case, it was an appalling state of affairs.

Where there was no need for seduction, there was no real interest for him and he'd quickly tired of his wanton little chambermaid. Pretorius felt they'd surpassed themselves but their achievement – if Justine could be called such – wasn't to Frankenstein's liking at all. He was bored. He wanted his old life back, with his meek, sexually inhibited lady patients. The ones who required a great deal of careful manipulation before they would even dream of spreading themselves lasciviously and demanding that he fuck them.

But even they seemed to be deserting him. Lillian Wingate had required three separate visits before she could be coaxed out of her underthings. Now, just when her surrender was within his grasp, she suddenly had more important things to do than see him. And Sylvia. Rich, reliable Sylvia who at least had the decency to *pretend* that he was taking advantage of her. She'd cancelled their last two appointments and postponed things indefinitely. Could she have found a new lover?

He glared at his empty brandy glass, recalling the night he and Pretorius had toasted their partnership, the future and their ambition to create the perfect woman. One didn't always achieve success on the first attempt; that was what experimentation was all about, after all. His first attempt had been a failure and now his second was proving to be one as well. No matter. He would adapt his methods, refine the formulae and try again when the opportunity presented itself. However, in the meantime he still needed money and his source of income was suddenly and inexplicably drying up.

He didn't want to become so desperate that he was forced to offer his services indiscriminately, tending to any and every lonely female in the city. He wasn't in it for charitable rewards. If he wasn't careful he'd have a queue of Gwendolyn Merrydales outside his door.

Perhaps he could send Justine round with calling cards to his regular patients. A little nudge to remind them what they were missing, a little temptation to spur them to come see him again. That was assuming he could persuade her to perform such a menial task, of course. He'd made a mistake in letting her get ideas above her station. Now she was more of a guest than a servant. An ungrateful guest who came and went as she pleased and repaid his kindness with deception and mockery.

He shoved himself to his feet and pressed the heels of his hands against his brow. There was no sense in letting it get to him. Justine was as he'd made her: wild and unfettered. Well, a wild animal in captivity must be tamed. And an experiment gone wrong must be put right. He could and would remedy both.

When Justine deigned to reappear he'd give her a piece of his mind. If necessary he would tell her the truth about herself and see how she liked that. Then there would be no need for any pretence. She was his creation and he her master. And whether she liked it or not, she would do as he said from now on. She would go obediently back to the laboratory with him and submit to further experiments until he had reformed her character to his liking. Pretorius would help him. When they were done she would be docile and obedient once more. And most of all grateful.

Something caught his eye at the edge of the fireplace and he crouched down to see what it was. A fragment of one of the notes had escaped the flames. He could just make out the words 'do hope' and 'forgive'.

With an acid smile he plucked the scrap of paper from the hearth and dropped it back into the fire where it was instantly consumed.

CHAPTER NINE

A New Acquaintance

The evening was crisp and clear and the stars winked like co-conspirators as Justine waved farewell to the figure in the window and stepped into the waiting carriage. She looked as grand as any lady in her russet velvet gown and cloak, a gift from Sylvia. The new clothes were very warm and comfortable, but Justine did not feel the cold in any case. The only chill she ever felt was the one she was returning home to. Frankenstein barely spared her a glance these days. He was like a cuckolded husband, glowering at a wife he couldn't control, who wouldn't conform to his idea of what a wife should be.

Ah, except that she was not his wife. Nor had that ever been his intent. He had saved her from the river for some secret purpose of his own but there was no way he could have foreseen what the process would do to her. Daisy had told her she was Frankenstein's maid before the accident. And he seemed to expect her to be happy returning to that lowly position. Making his bed, fetching his tea, answering the door to his patients.

But the experience had changed her. From what, she didn't know, as her memory had never returned. Like a girl in a fairy tale, she had gone to sleep a cat and woken as a tiger. One with keen eyes and bright shining fangs and sharp claws. What she did know was that she had a ravenous sexual appetite that her master couldn't satisfy. He didn't even seem interested in trying. Daisy was more than willing but for some reason Frankenstein saw her as a threat. Justine could sense his disquiet and she didn't believe for one minute that it was because he was concerned that people would talk. If he truly had no idea of his own reputation then he was the one with amnesia, not her.

In the weeks that followed Justine's 'rescue' he had changed too. At first he had treated her as something between a patient and a pet. Now she was something else to him entirely. Something that unnerved and even angered him.

Lulled by the rocking of the carriage, Justine listened to the horses' hooves on the cobblestones and watched the frost-dappled city glide past the window. Her flesh still tingled from the night's exertions. The rich widow was amusing but Justine would have to drop her soon. Of course, Sylvia was fully aware that she was being used, just as she was using Justine. How Frankenstein would gloat with conceit were he to know he was at the centre of their little trysts, the sun two conniving moons revolved around. But Justine knew him better than Sylvia did. Jealousy and possessiveness he could feel, certainly, and even passion. But love? Never.

He tolerated her romance with Daisy but he had no idea what else she got up to. Sylvia had sent him a note to apologise for her absence and Justine had asked the American girl to do the same. The poor wretch had been married off to a handsome man who was too arrogant to recognise that his wife's true desire lay not with a husband but with a wife of her own. Justine had immediately seen the combination of lust and sorrow in her eyes when she had opened the door to her on her first visit to Dr Frankenstein. And a few nights later Justine had slipped into Lillian Wingate's bed and shown her things the American beauty had never dreamt possible. It was only a taste of things to come, however. She fully intended to have both Mr and Mrs Wingate before she was through – preferably at the same time. Someone had to see to her needs and, if Frankenstein refused to do so, she would seek her own remedies.

When at last the tall buildings of Guy's Hospital hove into view, Justine knocked against the roof of the carriage to make the driver stop. She didn't want Frankenstein to see her return in Sylvia's carriage and she certainly didn't want him to see her in her fine new gown. Not yet anyway. Besides, it was a lovely evening and she fancied a walk along the river. The driver handed her out as he would any lady and tipped his hat to her before climbing back up into his seat. He flicked his whip over the horses' backs and they gave a whinny and trotted away.

Justine made her way to the bridge and stood gazing down at the river. Crusts of ice had formed along the banks but the river itself was undeterred by the cold. It slithered below her like a snake, enfolding the city in its coils. To think that she had ever stood here, breaking her heart in two like a silly romantic child! Whoever that girl was, she truly *had* met her end in those icy depths and the woman that had emerged to take her place was superior in every way.

After a while her keen senses told her she was being watched and she cocked her head slightly, listening for the telltale footsteps of a thief. But what she heard was not the step of a pickpocket's shoe; rather it was the rustle of finely tailored garments. The night was so still it carried the sound to her from the opposite side of the river. She spied her watcher at once and became intrigued.

His silhouette marked him as a gentleman, dressed in fine clothes. He was tall and bore himself with confidence. A man of learning and sophistication. As he drew nearer she could see that he was strikingly handsome, with strong chiselled features. A thin scar ran the length of one sharp cheekbone and she thrilled at the idea that he had acquired it in a duel. She put his age at a little more than her own and met his eyes as he approached her. He removed his top hat and made her a little bow, his red-lined opera cape swirling about him.

Justine inclined her head to him, returning his theatrical greeting. 'Good evening to you, sir,' she said, determined that she should be the first to speak, to show that she was not a simpering fool like other ladies he might know.

He smiled, his eyes searching her face, doubtless sizing her up as a conquest. But he surprised her when he said nothing. No trifling comment on the weather, no patronising astonishment that she should be out alone at night. He boldly placed himself beside her and peered down at the water, following its meandering course into the distance with his piercing gaze.

Taken aback, Justine didn't know what to do next. A proper lady should take offence and flounce off in a huff at his presumption. But Justine had no time for such ridiculous games. Society imposed so many elaborate and prescriptive rules for encounters with the opposite sex. A lady must be haughty and unapproachable, chaste and prim, while a gentleman must be gallant and deferential in the face of it. But for all their brittle posturing, such ladies could shatter at a single harsh word, swoon at the slightest breach of etiquette. It was an absurd charade and Justine would have no part of it. Already she was unlike any other woman of her time. Neither servant nor mistress, she was not subject to the whims of class distinction or societal rules of engagement. She was a creature all her own, and she determined to make the most of her unique situation. Frankenstein had taught her that if nothing else.

She looked her companion up and down and liked what she saw. Her lady lovers gave her pleasure enough, with their eager fingers and tongues, but they didn't set Justine's pulse racing the way this man did. Her body recalled the powerful sensations her master had wrung from her body, the exquisite feeling of being tightly bound and then unbound. Awakened. Alive.

Since then she had fully indulged her hunger, seeking new thrills only to be left wanting more. She had taken what knowledge she could from her master before realising there was nothing else he could teach her. He expected her to be content with her menial station as his chambermaid, but he had no idea of her potential. Were he a man of true ambition, he might exploit her fully. Alas, he was weakened by his own lust, a prosaic lust for power and wealth over experience. Justine had surpassed him.

With the acute awareness of a predatory animal, Justine felt the body heat of the man beside her. Indeed, she could smell him. His heady, musky scent was mingled with that of old books and something sharp and piquant, something chemical. She knew those smells. She opened her mouth to say something but he addressed her first, as though answering her unspoken question.

'We have an acquaintance in common.'

'Have we?'

'Dr Frankenstein.'

It was the last thing she had been expecting him to say. Her companion turned to her, smiling, and she fought to keep the surprise from her face.

'I see.' A little smirk nudged the corners of her mouth. 'You are someone's husband then?'

Laughing, he held up his left hand to show the lack of a wedding band. 'Dear me, no. But I do know his game.' He winked.

Intrigued, Justine gazed at him, waiting for him to explain.

'I'm one of his medical students,' the man said at last.

A student! That explained the smells. He was watching her face closely, as though overhearing her thoughts, and she likewise studied him. Somehow she couldn't picture him poring over books and dissection tables. Indeed, she had the distinct sense that, like her, he already knew more than his teachers. A man of the world, then. She smiled and peeled off her glove, offering him her hand.

'Justine. I'm – a friend of the family.'

'William,' he said. 'A pleasure to meet you.' He took her hand and raised it to his lips. His green eyes gleamed as he bent to kiss the bare flesh and she was sure she felt the tip of his tongue against her knuckle.

A warm thrill ran through her and she thought of the things he must have seen at Frankenstein's lectures. Specifically she imagined him peering down at one of his demonstration subjects, the girl's body stripped and displayed, then teased into arousal he could claim was hysteria and therefore 'cure' her of. Perhaps he had even seen Daisy.

'I would quite like being at one of those lectures,' Justine said with a mischievous grin.

'A woman would never be allowed in.'

'Oh, I didn't mean as an observer.'

William's eyes shone in the moonlight. 'I see. Do you suffer from the affliction he has made his speciality?'

'I wouldn't use the word "suffer". Rather, I have, shall we say, appetites? Much like those of a man, I'm told.'

'Told by whom?'

'By our mutual acquaintance. Among others.'

'That's unusual in a lady,' he said. 'So *I'm* told.'

Justine felt her breath catch as he moved closer to her. He stared into her eyes with a frankness that made her feel exposed, as though he could see straight into her mind.

'I've been watching you,' he said.

Her heart fluttered. 'Tracking' was what he really meant. As though he were a hunter and she a rare animal to be captured and displayed. She closed her eyes as he slipped his arm around her waist, pulling her up against him. He guided her hand to the hardness in his trousers. Her sex throbbed insistently. She closed her hand around the bulge and felt it swell and twitch in response to her touch. He exhaled softly, his breath warm against her throat.

Trembling, she squeezed him harder and was rewarded with a rough kiss. He took her face in his hands and pressed his mouth to hers, plunging his tongue between her lips. When he finally tore away he took her firmly by the arm, leading her across the bridge and into a cluster of small trees. The light from the streetlamp fell just short of the trees and she surrendered as he backed her into the shadows and pushed her to her knees in the grass. Frost crunched beneath her. She quickly unfastened his trousers and freed his cock.

She was desperate to taste it and even more desperate to feel it in her cunt. But she forced herself to savour the moment, casting off her other glove and encouraging him to his full length with her fingers. Wrapping her hand around the base, she squeezed with all her might and thrilled to his responses. His cock throbbed, hardening even more. Still clutching it tightly, she kissed the sensitive tip, then fluttered her tongue against the little ridge just below it, enjoying his moans of pleasure. He tasted rich and salty. She dragged her tongue along the length of his cock, teasing herself as much as him.

At last she opened her mouth and took him in,

wrapping her lips around the shaft and swallowing him slowly, inch by inch. William twisted his hands in her hair, disarranging it as he rocked his hips against her, pushing himself in and out, as deep as he could go.

After a little while his legs began to tremble with the effort and Justine pulled away. She didn't want him to finish yet. She lay back on the grass, not caring if she ruined her new clothes. Everything and everyone else was instantly forgotten. This man was her whole world.

His eyes glittered as he knelt before her and spread her legs wide. He took his time lifting first her skirt, then her petticoats one by one, while she shuddered in an ecstasy of anticipation. He unlaced her drawers and peeled them down to her ankles, where they caught in a tangle round her feet. With a wicked smile William roughly forced her knees apart, exposing her warm sex to the icy night and the moonlight.

Justine gasped and threw her head back as he touched her, first stroking her with his fingers and then pressing his palm against the wetness he found there. He moved his hand in slow circles, stimulating her unbearably before at last slipping a finger inside her. He swirled it around and she clutched at the grass on either side of her, not knowing what to do with her hands. She suddenly longed to be restrained, to be held down and ravished as Frankenstein had held her down that first night in the laboratory. Here was a man worthy of her surrender.

No sooner had she had the thought than he seized her slim wrists and pinned them against the ground. She cried out in surprise as she heard a seam rip in one of her sleeves. William ignored it, silencing her with another bruising kiss and manoeuvring himself into position. Justine strained towards him, begging him with her body. His eyes met hers then and he plunged himself inside, thrusting in up to the hilt. The muscles of her sex contracted around his cock, drawing him in and clenching as though she could hold him there. Again he seemed to know exactly what she wanted for he remained still, allowing her to savour the feeling of being filled by him.

'Oh please,' she gasped at last. 'Please fuck me.'

He did. Each thrust was deep and powerful, so intense she had to grit her teeth to stifle her cries. Her body was melting the frost beneath them and the dampness and the sharp smell of the grass made her feel wild and bestial. The river lapped at its icy banks and in the distance an owl screeched. A hackney rattled across the bridge, its occupants oblivious to the fact that a well-dressed gentleman was fucking a lady on the cold hard ground only a few yards away.

William found a steady rhythm, each stroke making her shudder with pleasure. At last he released her wrists and Justine twined her fingers through his hair, pulling his face down to hers for another kiss. He kissed a trail down her throat, kneading her breasts through the velvet of her dress and the chemise beneath. Justine arched her back, presenting herself to him. He hooked his fingers into her décolletage and hauled the fabric down, freeing her breasts from their confinement. Her nipples stiffened instantly in the frigid air and she guided his mouth to them, gasping as he pressed her breasts together, kissing first one, then the other. When his tongue found her nipples she felt a rush of euphoria that told her she wasn't far from climax.

He began to fuck her harder then, and faster, mauling her breasts with his hands as he pounded in and out of her. His fingers closed around her nipples, pinching them, and then he drove himself in with one long delicious thrust. His body convulsed with the force of his climax and Justine felt the hot jets of his seed pulsing into her. She closed her eyes, feeling his orgasm along with him. Every little throb and twitch seemed to feed directly into her, keeping her stimulated and vibrating.

William gazed down at her and his expression made her weak with pleasure. As he eased himself out, she imagined the scandalous sight she must present – her dress torn, her drawers wound about her ankles, her breasts and sex lewdly displayed for anyone to see. It only excited her more.

Without a word William slid his hand up between her legs, stroking the little bud of her clitoris with his fingers. With his other hand he continued to play with her nipples, making her jump with each little tweak. The movement of his fingers on her clit increased, growing faster. Justine threw her head back, drawing short ragged breaths as the focused stimulation to her most sensitive parts finally pushed her over the edge. She came loudly, wildly, thrashing in the frozen grass, lost to the sublime ecstasy of his touch.

A shower of stars sparkled behind her eyes and it seemed a blissful eternity before the waves of pleasure began to fade. Finally, she drifted back to reality and for a moment she was afraid to open her eyes lest she find William gone. Or worse – never there at all. She didn't doubt her vivid imagination capable of such a cruel trick. But he was there. He was real. And she was his completely.

'That was … I've never …' She didn't know what to say.

'I know,' he said, smiling. 'I feel the same.'

She looked down at herself and gave a rueful little laugh. 'How am I ever to get home like this? If anyone should see me, they'd think I'd been assaulted!'

William rose and helped her to her feet. He held her skirts up for her while she adjusted her drawers. Although they served little purpose, exposing more than they concealed, she couldn't very well leave them here. The dress, she knew, was ruined. She couldn't tug the neckline back into any semblance of decency.

'Perhaps my cloak will hide the damage,' she said. But it too was torn and stained from the grass.

'Allow me,' William said, removing his own and passing it round her shoulders. 'It's the least I can do. Although you really shouldn't go home like that.'

'Oh, there won't be any trouble about it,' she said blithely, knowing he could see through the lie. Part of her loved the idea of Frankenstein seeing her in such a scandalous state, of taunting him with her debauchery. But he didn't deserve to play any part in this extraordinary night's adventure. In one evening, everything had changed.

William was watching her steadily, as though reading her thoughts. 'I have rooms nearby,' he said, 'where you would be more than welcome.'

Something in his eyes both reassured and unsettled her. She had the strangest sense that he'd known her all her life, as though they were bound by some dark magic.

As though they were made for one another.

'Who are you?' she asked, finally succumbing to the queerness of the encounter.

He touched her cheek with casual affection. 'Simply a man who knows a few tricks,' he said, but the gleam in his eye hinted at extraordinary secrets. He held out his arm. 'Shall we go?'

She smiled and hooked her arm through his. She liked the thought of falling asleep in his arms, of waking to more of his attentions, of finding out those secrets for herself.

CHAPTER TEN

Pleasure Slave

Daisy's hands wandered lazily over her skin, trying to re-create the feel of Justine's touch. Her head was filled with endless variations on their encounters. The nights of wild passion in Justine's bed. Spontaneous stolen moments behind trees, in alleyways and one bold afternoon in Daisy's father's bookshop.

Daisy sighed as she pushed a finger inside her own slippery folds, imagining that it was Justine penetrating her so rigorously, so expertly. With her other hand she teased the little knot of her clitoris, recalling the sensation of Justine's tongue there, hot and eager.

She was back in her oldest and most enduring fantasy. She had been captured, along with a bevy of other girls, and taken by ship to a foreign land. There she stood in a line with the others along a platform in a dusty market square. Men called out in a strange language and one by one each girl was led to the front of the platform and made to undress. Those who disobeyed were whipped.

When it was Daisy's turn she went where she was led and her clothes were forcibly removed with no resistance from her. She stood there, naked in the heat of the unfamiliar sun, exposed to the eyes of all the men before her. The auctioneer made her turn this way and that and she trembled with fear as he displayed her to the crowd. He forced her mouth open and peered inside at her teeth as though it were a horse and not a girl he was buying. He stroked the skin of her thigh. He squeezed her breasts roughly. He bent her over and parted her cheeks. He made her lift first one bare foot, then the other, to inspect them.

Daisy's eyes filled with tears of humiliation and yet she couldn't help the fact that his attentions made her wet with desire. With her back to the crowd she gazed along the line at her sisters in slavery. They were all so beautiful; it was little wonder someone wanted to collect them like butterflies.

The auctioneer's rough hands turned her around again and then there was the clamour of voices as men from the crowd shouted out their price for her. Despite her terror she was caught up in the frenzy of the auction. At last a price was agreed with someone she couldn't see and she was bustled off the platform and taken away.

The place in which she found herself was an opulent

room scented with jasmine. It was draped with lavish tapestries and furnished with plush cushions. Two burly men in loincloths guarded the curtained entrance but inside the room was populated only by women. The most exotic women she had ever seen. They wore gleaming jewels and gossamer silks in the most fantastic colours. Daisy was dressed similarly. There was a luxurious sunken bath in the centre of the room and several women frolicked in it, splashing each other and laughing.

As Daisy went among the others she suddenly felt a tug at her sleeve. She turned and there was Justine, draped in scarlet, her dark hair entwined with flowers and her eyes as deep as any mystery.

I can show you things that will make you fly.

Daisy sighed with pleasure as Justine slipped the filmy garments from Daisy's shoulders and caressed her bared breasts, dipping her head to kiss each dusky pink nipple. And then her lips found Daisy's and their tongues met, entwining wetly. Daisy tasted exotic spices.

And then Justine was leading her away, guiding her naked down a long elegant corridor to a magnificent bedchamber. There the sultan stood waiting, watching, as Justine positioned Daisy between two marble columns in the centre of the room. Spreading Daisy's arms out to the sides, she fastened her wrists into the shackles that hung there. Daisy strained towards Justine, trying to reach her, to kiss her, to bury her face in her soft dark hair. But Justine edged away, smiling that wicked, beguiling smile.

Behind her Daisy heard the soft slap of bare feet on the marble floor and then there was the press of warm flesh against her back. The sultan's strong arms encircled her, pulling her back against the hardness she could now feel nudging insistently against her sex.

Daisy resisted only slightly, pulling at the shackles and casting a pleading look towards Justine. The chains held her fast and she felt feverish with excitement as she realised just how helpless she was. But she was a pleasure slave. It was her duty to please.

Justine returned to her, teasing her with kisses and caresses, while the sultan's cock grew ever harder against Daisy's sex. She wanted them both. Justine's tenderness and the sultan's cruelty. The roughness of a man and the comfort of a woman. Suddenly the sultan fisted a hand firmly in Daisy's hair and pulled her head back. Daisy cried out as his cock slid easily inside her and then Justine silenced her with a kiss.

The sultan's hands clutched her breasts from behind, kneading her roughly and tweaking her nipples as he thrust in and out of her. And all the while Justine toyed with her from the front, kissing her, nipping at her throat, stroking her thighs. Daisy surrendered to the confusion of male and female hands on her at the same time, writhing helplessly in her chains as she urged them both on.

Justine's cool hands danced across Daisy's skin, slowly making their way down to where Daisy wanted them most. The sultan fucked her hard from behind while Justine drew her fingers lightly over her belly and down to where her thighs branched. Daisy's legs trembled with the effort of staying upright and she whimpered as Justine at last reached her clitoris. She touched it with maddening delicacy and Daisy moaned, urging her on, begging for more.

The pounding cock filled her and withdrew, again and again, its rhythm slowing as the sultan neared climax. His hands squeezed her breasts even harder and he pinched her nipples viciously, making her yelp as he rolled them between thumb and forefinger. Her mingled cries of pain and pleasure seemed to please him and only then did Justine crouch down to press her lips against Daisy's sex, fluttering her tongue against her clit as the sultan stiffened behind her with a long low moan. As he came, so did Daisy, in an ecstatic burst that made the chains jingle as the convulsions rocked her both within and without.

Justine stayed where she was, sucking the sensitive organ into her mouth to tease it further with her tongue. Daisy cried out with helpless abandon until the orgasm had peaked and at last begun to subside. Then she hung limp in her bonds until her tormentors released her and let her curl up at their feet in the blissful afterglow.

Daisy panted as the fantasy dissipated and she hoped

she hadn't cried out where anyone could hear. She turned onto her side and pulled the blankets around herself tightly, cocooning herself as she pressed her legs together to intensify the dwindling spasms of her climax.

The fantasy had come from a book on Orientalist paintings. Lush representations of harems and slave markets that captured the mysteries of the East. The pictures hinted at all manner of strange rituals. A coiled whip here, a jar of ointment there, a room full of beautiful, exotic women and a scowling man inspecting a naked girl on an auction block. It had always been a private, secret world for her. Now Justine was there with her. She was everywhere Daisy went now, even in her most intimate thoughts. Justine had bewitched her. Enslaved her.

She had decided never to tell Justine about the past. Certainly not about Ralph, who had never deserved her love in the first place. She was determined to protect her friend from those who would do her harm. Her heart swelled with so many emotions she didn't know how to process them all. One thing was certain. She would not let Frankenstein keep Justine shut away from the world and especially not from her.

With a sigh Daisy closed her eyes and smiled. 'Justine,' she whispered, just to say her name. Come what may, they would be together.

CHAPTER ELEVEN

Questions

William's arms were still around her when she woke the next morning. The night had been filled with warmth and wetness, with hard thrusts and soft sighs, whispers and screams.

His lips moved against her ear and Justine murmured sleepily as she pressed back against him, not wanting him to release her. She suspected he had been awake for a while, holding her. Perhaps listening to her deep, easy breathing as she slept. Watching her eyelids flutter as she dreamed.

His bedroom was small, but he filled it with his presence the way a king inhabited a castle. In the living area was a table strewn with books and papers. An anatomy text was splayed open and a paperweight partially obscured a diagram of the human form. Justine had seen similar drawings in Frankenstein's rooms. The place looked the way she had expected a student's quarters to look.

There was no need for modesty with William. She had removed her torn and tattered garments, and sat naked on the edge of his bed as she sipped the wine he offered her and waited for his clothes to join hers on the floor. He obliged and she admired his lean and wiry physique in the firelight. In the glow of the flames he was like a statue cast in bronze. He had likewise made her parade her charms for him and she had enjoyed the freedom of showing herself off. His keen eyes took in every detail. His hands soon followed.

Justine's body ached after the night's exertions. Like her, William seemed to have an unending hunger for sex and she had no idea how many times he had plunged himself inside her and made her beg for more. Even now, after hours of feasting on each other, she could feel him growing hard against her bottom.

'Have you not had your fill *yet*?' she asked with an incredulous laugh.

'I might ask the same of you.' He slipped a hand between her legs and tutted at the wetness he found there, the wetness that was always there.

She purred and angled herself so that he could slide into her again and this time he fucked her slowly, gently, like a lover. Afterwards she dozed in his arms before the clatter of a cart outside broke the spell.

'I should go,' she said with a regretful sigh.

'Why?'

His question gave her pause. Yes, *why* must she? Because Frankenstein would be out of his mind with fury at her indiscretion? Why should she trouble herself about that? He and his friend Pretorius had both praised her spirit and in the beginning at least Frankenstein had seemed to enjoy her lack of inhibitions. According to Daisy, she hadn't always been so bold. The accident had altered her personality as it had stolen her memory. But now there was no more praise for her. Now there was only scowling displeasure and attempts to control her. Now there was only the lowly position he expected her to be content with.

'I don't know,' she said at last. 'But I must.'

William rolled her over to face him and his eyes narrowed as he regarded her seriously. 'Justine, you don't owe him anything.'

She pulled away from him, frowning. 'He saved my life.'

William's lips parted as though he were about to speak. He said nothing, but a shadow seemed to darken his face. Justine stared at his scar and for a moment she wondered if Frankenstein had been the other duellist. But she quickly dismissed the thought. She couldn't see her master crossing swords with anyone, especially not one of his medical students.

'You're too clever,' William said, choosing his words carefully. 'Too resourceful. You don't belong there, shut up in that cold dark house, playing maid to a man who doesn't appreciate your special talents.'

She tried not to let her surprise show. She'd told William last night that she was a friend of the family. She must have slipped and given herself away at some point. It hardly mattered. In her heart she agreed with William, yet she still felt strangely bound to her master.

'But I *am* his maid,' she said sadly. 'And I do owe him my life.'

Again a shadow flickered across William's face. Did he know something he wasn't telling her? Something about her past perhaps? She stared at him, searching his face. Something was nagging at her, some fragment of memory. 'Do I know you?' she asked at last.

He laughed good-naturedly. 'A fine question to ask someone you've spent the last twenty-four lust-filled hours with!'

She ignored the jest and continued to study him, narrowing her eyes as the feeling of déjà vu washed over her. 'There's something so … familiar about you. I felt it last night but now it's even stronger.'

William met her stare with a piercing gaze of his own, his eyes boring into her as they searched for something in her eyes. Then he sat up suddenly and clasped both her hands, pulling her up with him. 'Come with me,' he said. 'Run away. I can promise you a life of pleasure and happiness for the rest of your days. A life where you will never be taken for granted, never forced to do anything you don't want to do.'

His intensity disturbed her and she drew back from him a little. 'I couldn't betray him like that.'

'Couldn't you?' His jaw clenched. 'I see. Perhaps you enjoy being his slave. Making his bed, tidying his house, fetching his slippers. Or perhaps your betrayals are merely limited to seducing other women.'

Justine's eyes flashed. 'How dare you? If you mean Daisy, I –'

'I do not mean Daisy,' he said coolly. 'I mean Mrs Sylvia Leigh-Hunt. I mean Mrs Lillian Wingate. And however many other of his so-called "patients" you've turned against him without arousing his suspicions. Yes, I know all about it. Don't look so shocked.'

Justine gaped at him, not knowing what to say. Had he been following her all this time, spying on her? To what purpose?

William held up his hand. 'Now, before you curse me for a villain, listen to me. There are things about your master that you don't know. Things that you *ought* to know.'

'Tell me, then,' she said haughtily.

He shook his head. 'No. You would never believe me if I told you. You must find out for yourself.'

'I see. More riddles. Presumably you have some sordid history with him yourself, then.'

He laughed, a bitter, humourless sound. 'You could say that.'

She searched his face for signs that he was just toying with her but he looked absolutely sincere. Like a man with a dark past of which he dared not speak. He saw her watching him and added, 'Your secrets are bound up with mine.'

'Can you at least tell me what I'm looking for, then?'

'Search his laboratory,' William said. 'Look for a journal. Notes about certain experiments.'

Justine remembered seeing a journal. It was the day after Frankenstein had rescued her, the day he and Pretorius had tested all her sensations. He had recorded all her responses in a heavy leather-bound volume.

'Very well,' she said cautiously, 'I'll see what I can find.'

William allowed the hard line of his jaw to relax as he smiled at her. 'You'll want to see me again when you're done. I'll tell you everything I know then.'

Justine offered him an uneasy smile of her own. There was nothing in the world she wanted more than to spend the rest of her days with him, in his arms, in his bed. Why, then, did she feel so inexplicably bound to the man who had shown her kindness and then brushed her aside? Had her master simply got tired of her? If so, why was he so determined to keep her under his thumb? And what

131

would become of Daisy if she absconded with William? She couldn't leave her dearest friend behind.

She shook her head to clear it. Such questions could wait. They would have to.

She glanced over at the torn remnants of her clothes and frowned. The new gown Sylvia had given her was ruined, as was the velvet cloak. For all her defence of Frankenstein, she didn't want him to know where she'd been or what she'd been up to. She knew he'd be furious that she'd stayed out all night. Perhaps he'd even been genuinely worried about her. But under no circumstances must she come slinking back the next morning looking like the victim of an animal attack.

'I'm afraid I've nothing for you to wear,' William said with a sheepish grin. 'Unless … Yes, of course!' He climbed out of bed and opened the small wardrobe in the corner of the room. He took a white shirt from it and held it up to her.

'If you're suggesting that I try and pass for a man …'

He laughed. 'Of course not! But it's obvious you've been out all night with *someone*. Better this than the remnants of a fancy gown that clearly wasn't yours to begin with. A gown he might even recognise.'

Warming to the sport of it, Justine allowed him to dress her, helping her step into a pair of dark-brown trousers. He tore a long strip of velvet from her cloak and cinched it tight around the waistband of the trousers to hold them in place. The shirt hung on her as though she were a child but the frock coat he draped around her shoulders swallowed her whole, concealing any hint of the feminine shape beneath.

William stepped back to admire his handiwork and a lascivious smile played at the corners of his mouth.

'What's so funny?' Justine asked.

'Oh, nothing. My tastes only run to the fairer sex, I'm afraid, but for you I'd make an exception.'

Her sex tingled at that and for a moment she entertained the thought of staying to explore the possibilities. But then she shook her head with a determined laugh. 'You're incorrigible.'

'We're the same, you and I.' He kissed her deeply and when he pulled away his face had clouded again. 'Very soon you'll see just how alike we are.'

His words had the sense of ill omen about them and she heard them echoing in her head all the way home.

CHAPTER TWELVE

Secrets

'And where have you been all night?'

Justine closed her eyes and took a deep breath as the approaching tap of footsteps grew louder. She arranged her features into a coquettish smile and turned to face her master. Her heart hadn't slowed its pounding since she'd opened the front door and it was all she could do to suppress her nervousness. She'd never seen him so angry.

'I went for a walk,' she said. It had become her standard excuse. Normally, she delivered it with flippant nonchalance, as though it were none of his business. This morning her tone was a little more subdued.

Frankenstein's eyes widened as he took in her appearance. 'What are you wearing?' Before she could speak, he snarled, 'I suppose this was Daisy's idea.'

Justine didn't want to implicate her friend but it offered her the perfect cover. 'Yes, as a matter of fact.' She forced herself to laugh, a free and easy sound that had once come so naturally to her. She gave a little twirl to show off her gentleman's attire. 'We thought it might be fun to dress up.'

He shook his head in disgust and for a moment anger flared within her and she was tempted to tell him exactly what she'd been up to and with whom. She resisted the urge, however, battling a storm of conflicting feelings.

In the beginning she had loved him. Her master, her saviour. She had been eager to please him – and, in so doing, please herself – but then he had cast her aside. Relegated her to the menial position she had apparently occupied before her misadventure in the river. Strangest of all was the sense that he was wary of her, that at times he even feared her.

She had found comfort in the arms of Daisy, then in those of other ladies. It had been her half-formed plan to make him jealous, to make him turn his attentions back to her. But then she met William and everything changed.

When William had planted doubts in her mind about Frankenstein, she had surprised herself by bristling in her master's defence despite his careless treatment of her. But the truth was that she did feel bound to him. Joined almost as if in marriage.

There are things about your master that you don't know.

She was afraid to learn the truth, but now, more

than ever, she knew that she must. Whatever his secrets were, she must know them. Then and only then could she decide how to proceed. But she mustn't upset the balance with Frankenstein. Not yet anyway. She had to make the peace.

'I'm sorry, sir,' she murmured, lowering her head and clasping her hands behind her back in a show of remorse. 'It was terribly thoughtless of me.'

Although she could only see him from the waist down, his body language changed markedly. He relaxed and drew a deep breath, releasing it in a long sigh. Then he took her face between his hands and lifted her head until their eyes met.

'Justine,' he said, shaking his head. 'You can't simply do as you please without a care for the danger involved.'

The only danger, she thought, is to you.

'I know, sir. I shouldn't risk scandal like that. It could ruin your reputation.'

'Absolutely,' he said with relief. He seemed as keen as she was to embrace the pretence that this was all about the appearance of respectability, but she knew now that it was because he had his own secrets to keep from her. As soon as she got the chance she would find out what they were. Already she had a plan.

She glanced down at herself and offered him a sheepish grin. 'I suppose I had better find something more appropriate to wear.'

'Yes, I think that would be wise.'

As she climbed the stairs to her room she felt his eyes on her. Did he suspect her of anything other than brazen indiscretion? She could only hope he didn't. Once she knew what he was hiding it would no longer matter. She opened and closed the door to her room and then waited on the landing until she heard him go into his study. Satisfied that he didn't suspect anything, she hurriedly stripped out of William's clothes and put on her black dress and pinafore. She tucked her hair up into her mob cap and stared at her reflection in wonder. Only yesterday she had worn a lady's fine velvet gown. The transformation from lady to gentleman and now to chambermaid was striking. If only she could do without clothes entirely! With a wry smile she slipped back out of the room.

She tiptoed out onto the landing and down the stairs, listening for Frankenstein all the while. But his study door remained firmly shut. Without a sound she slipped into the kitchen and out the back door. She only needed a moment.

There was a newsboy on the corner, shouting out the day's headline and handing out copies of the London *Times* for threepence.

'You, there,' she hissed. 'Boy!'

The boy turned, clutching his sheaf of papers as though he thought she might steal them.

'I've got a job for you,' she said.

He eyed her mistrustfully until he saw the sixpenny piece she was offering him. Then a hungry look replaced the scepticism and he held out his hand greedily. The gloves he wore were filthy and had unravelled to expose his fingers, which were bright red from the cold.

'What's the job? I ain't gonna pinch no swell's pocket watch for you.'

'It's nothing like that at all. In fact, it's easy. I want you to go round to the front door of number nineteen and ring the bell. I'll answer it but you must pretend you've never seen me before. Say you have an urgent message for Dr Frankenstein, that his friend Dr Pretorius needs to see him at once. Can you remember all of that?'

'That's really all I have to do?' he asked incredulously.

'That's all.'

The boy smiled and pocketed the sixpence, clearly delighted to be earning so much for so little. The coin would go some way towards keeping him warm. For a little while anyway. 'You can count on me,' he said earnestly, then added 'miss' for good measure.

Justine hurried back to the house. 'Just give me a few minutes!' she called.

Frankenstein's study door was still shut when she returned and she spent the next ten minutes pacing from the kitchen to the library and back again until the bell rang. She took her time reaching the front door, hoping the sound would have roused her master. With any luck he would be listening at the door of his study to see who'd come calling, no doubt prepared to leap out if he heard Daisy's voice.

Justine opened the door to the newsboy who loudly proclaimed that he had an urgent message for Dr Frankenstein.

On hearing his name, Frankenstein emerged from his study and came to the door. 'What is it?' he asked gruffly.

The boy played his part well and delivered the message as instructed. Frankenstein gave him tuppence for his trouble. Beaming with joy, the boy thanked him and scampered back to the street with a spring in his step. If any further duplicity should prove necessary, she knew she had a loyal accomplice.

'I hope it's nothing serious,' Justine said as she helped her master on with his coat. 'I like Dr Pretorius. He's a kind man.'

'I'm sure he's fine,' Frankenstein said, but there was concern in his voice. 'I don't know how long I'll be gone. But while I'm out ...'

Justine batted her lashes submissively. 'Yes, sir. I'll stay here. I promise.'

'Good girl.' He touched her cheek with something like affection. Not so long ago she would have thrilled to his touch. Now William was all she could think of. She waved to Frankenstein from the window, as though he were a soldier going off to war.

A slow smile spread across her face as she watched him out of sight. Then she mounted the stairs and made her way to the laboratory.

CHAPTER THIRTEEN

Female Treachery

Frankenstein alighted from the cab and hurried up the icy path to the little Georgian house where Pretorius lived. He rapped his cane against the front door. There was no answer. After some minutes he grew concerned and rapped again, louder. Finally he heard the scamper of footfalls and a flustered little maid answered. She blushed prettily when she saw who it was.

'Oh, Dr Frankenstein, sir,' she said, panting for breath. 'Please forgive me. Only I was just – making up the beds and I didn't hear –'

He waved away her excuse with an understanding smile. He knew only too well what had kept her so long. Her pinafore was askew and her hair was sticking out from under her cap in places. She hadn't even laced her shoes.

'It's quite all right,' he assured her. 'I believe Dr Pretorius sent for me?'

She looked puzzled. 'Did he?'

'Yes, I was told he needed to see me urgently.'

Still looking doubtful, she held the door open for him. 'Then you'd better come in.' After taking his coat, she led him into Pretorius's library and invited him to sit down. 'I'll just go and fetch him now, sir,' she said, hesitating in the doorway. 'I – er, won't be a moment.'

As soon as she closed the door behind her, it dawned on him why she'd been acting so peculiarly. If he had interrupted what he assumed he'd interrupted, there was little chance that Pretorius had sent for him. He frowned at the door as he tried to puzzle it out. Before long he heard footsteps and Pretorius flung open the library door, resplendent in a gaily coloured silk dressing gown. He was still knotting the sash as he came in and he didn't look pleased to see his friend.

'Frankenstein, what's this nonsense Polly tells me about me needing you urgently? I was right in the middle of something.'

All at once Frankenstein understood. He rose slowly to his feet. 'Justine,' he snarled, as though her name were an obscenity. 'That treacherous, conniving girl!'

Pretorius looked bewildered. 'What? My dear chap, what are you raving about? Why are you here?'

Frankenstein's face burned with fury and humiliation. 'I'm here,' he said, 'because I was tricked into coming here. Because someone wanted me out of the house. And I'm sure I can guess why.'

'Oh dear. I'm sorry to hear that, old chap. She is rather
... insatiable. I gather she has a lover?'

He nodded, scowling. 'Damn her. And damn Daisy
too!'

Pretorius quirked an eyebrow at that. 'Daisy?' Then
realisation dawned in his face. 'Ahhh. I see.'

'Yes. That wretched girl I hired for my last demonstration. I didn't realise they were friends. Now they're more
than that. Justine stayed out all night and came back this
morning wearing trousers and a bloody frock coat if you
can believe it. Said she and her little girlfriend had been
playing dress-up, as though they were children! Oh, she
made it up very sweetly: "I'm sorry, sir, how inconsiderate
of me, sir, it won't happen again, sir," but now I see.
Now I see ...' He clenched his fists in impotent rage as
he paced back and forth.

'Trousers?' Pretorius asked after a weighty pause. 'Did
you say trousers?'

'Yes. Shirt, coat and all. Heaven only knows where
they got them. It wouldn't surprise me if they waylaid
some poor customer in that shabby bookshop. Coshed
him, stripped him and left him to freeze in the alley.'

He looked up and the expression on his friend's face
stopped his tirade in its tracks. 'What is it?'

Pretorius laid a sympathetic hand on his shoulder.
'My good fellow, you don't mean to tell me you believed
that story?'

'Story?'

'I don't think it's the little Sapphist you need to worry about,' Pretorius said gently.

A moment's cold reflection and he had it. His head swam and all at once he felt lightheaded. 'Of course,' he said. 'What a fool I've been.' Anger and jealousy had blinded him to the obvious truth. Which had been staring him straight in the face this morning. No, the little strumpet hadn't been with Daisy; she'd been with another *man*. But who? Was he there with her now?

Pretorius gave a sigh and shook his head. 'Women, eh? Who can know their minds?'

'I have to go,' Frankenstein choked out, his voice as unsteady as his legs. 'I'll find out what her game is. And whoever her fancy man is, I swear I'll kill him.'

CHAPTER FOURTEEN

Revelation

Justine unlocked the laboratory with the spare key Frankenstein kept in the desk in his study. If he'd had any suspicion that she was up to no good, he'd surely have hidden it. Or perhaps it simply hadn't occurred to him that she would be so bold as to take it.

The laboratory door clicked open easily, like an invitation. She hadn't been inside for weeks and the room held strange memories for her. All of them good, all of them erotically charged. But now those happy memories were tainted by the dark and sinister veil that hung between her and her master.

In the centre of the room was the table where she had lain, splayed and ready, until he had at last pinned her down and fucked her. And against the far wall was the adjustable contraption where she had been strapped down and blindfolded while he and Pretorius experimented on her with different devices.

So much had changed in the days and weeks that had followed. She'd learnt so much, discovered things about herself she never could have imagined. She felt suffused with warmth and she pressed her legs together against the flood of memories. Her body ached for more. It was just as Frankenstein had said: her entire body was an erogenous zone. She never seemed to stop wanting stimulation. She craved it now, at this very moment. But now was not the time to indulge herself; she must focus on the task at hand.

Justine crossed to the roll-top desk and wasn't surprised to find it locked. No matter. She'd seen Frankenstein lock it that day with Pretorius, when she'd also seen him writing in the leather-bound journal. Unless he had moved it, the journal was in the top right-hand drawer and the key to unlock the roll-top was in a side drawer. Either he was very confident or very careless. In no time at all she had the book in her hands.

She opened the journal and turned to the first page. *Notes on Experimental Subject B*, it said in an elegant italic hand. *Justine Asher, chambermaid*. It wasn't long before her eyes widened with disbelief and then horror at what followed.

There was plenty she didn't understand. Long passages with detailed scientific and medical terminology she couldn't follow. But she understood the relevant bits. Again and again her eyes strayed to the water tank in the corner. It had always triggered a strange feeling in her. An alien familiarity, as though she'd spent considerable time there. And, according to Frankenstein's notes, she had.

She had asked him about it once and been told that it was an obsolete piece of equipment, a device similar in function to the Alleviator. Then he'd directed her attention elsewhere. At the time she hadn't thought anything of his haste to change the subject. Now, however, all his past actions were weighted with significance.

Subject seems unaffected by any change in temperature, although her skin retains an almost feverish warmth.

That was certainly true. It had puzzled her that others felt the cold while she herself did not. She had simply supposed herself to be hardier. If she had asked him why that was so, what would he have said? That it was a side effect of the 'accident'? That it was all in her mind? Whatever the excuse, she might have believed him.

Her rate of learning is astonishing. When I first hired Justine she could read only a little; now she absorbs information at an accelerated rate. If I were a superstitious man I might believe that the lightning had unlocked some ancient store of knowledge within her.

The lightning.

As she read on, clouds occasionally passed before the sun, altering the light that poured in through the skylight and illuminating the tank directly below it. Shadows sprang up around it, then faded as the sun reappeared.

Light glinted off the thin crust of ice and the still water beneath it. Justine saw her face in the glass of the tank, her snowsheen skin blazing in the reflected light from above. Again and again the image vanished and then re-materialised, like a conjuror's trick.

And just like that it came back to her. She remembered the lightning. She closed her eyes as everything fell into place. She remembered everything.

Ralph. The icy river. Frankenstein and Pretorius helping her out of the tank and unwinding the bandages from her newly reawakened body. She remembered what happened after that and she remembered what had gone before. The Alleviator. Being shaved. The tiny woman Pretorius kept in a cage, that he claimed to have grown like a flower in his own laboratory. Real. It was all real.

And as fantastic as it all was, it made sense. It answered all her questions. All except for one. She frowned at the first page again. *Experimental Subject B*. If she was Subject B, then ...

'Now you understand why I said you had to find out for yourself.'

She closed her eyes at the sound of William's voice. Of course. She went limp as he took her in his arms and the journal slid from her hand onto the stone floor.

'We're the same, you and I,' William said, kissing her.

Justine pressed her mouth against his, driven by more than just the hunger that had been engineered in her. She was desperate for contact, for connection. Communion. She knew at last who and what she truly was, but with it came the knowledge that there was only one other person who was like her in the world.

She understood everything now. Frankenstein didn't care about her. Perhaps he had once but now she was merely his creation. An interesting but troublesome little project that had got quite out of hand. His possessiveness didn't stem from any affection for her; it had simply been about keeping his activities secret from the outside world. Once he'd sampled her unique charms, he'd grown bored. She'd been too willing and eager for his liking. It was all there in his journal.

Subject is frustratingly single-minded. I must see if there is some way to temper her sex drive.

He preferred seducing meek and virginal young ladies to satisfying the unending lust of one who no longer had any sense of shame. No wonder he had been so provoked by her antics with Daisy.

'He made me this way,' she mused, thinking back on all her sexual exploits. The drive had never even been her own.

But William was smiling, his eyes suddenly playful. 'No, that's where you're wrong.'

'But it said in the notes,' Justine protested, pointing down at the book. 'Dr Pretorius – some formula in the water ...'

William shook his head. 'Dr Pretorius had nothing to do with *my* awakening,' he said, 'and you've seen what I can do.'

She had indeed. He was her perfect match. She stood drinking in his handsome face, his bright-green eyes. They danced with the same unearthly light Frankenstein had described in her. The light that meant there were still some things beyond his control.

'Then what is it? Why are we both … the way we are?'

He shrugged. 'A side effect of the reanimation process, perhaps? Who knows? All I know is that you're just like me. I certainly wasn't poisoned by any nymphomaniacal chemicals.'

Justine considered his words and her disquiet melted away. So there was something for which Frankenstein was not responsible after all. The lust was all her own. And William's.

'I'll come with you,' she said, smiling at William as she pressed her hands against his swelling crotch. 'For ever.'

He carried her to the table and sat her down on the smooth wood. Then he pushed his hands up underneath her skirt, slipping them through the slit in her drawers. His fingers teased her for a moment, tickling and spreading her, and then they were inside her. She gasped and threw her head back, gripping the edges of the table and forcing her legs as far apart as she could, offering herself. The last time she had been here, Frankenstein had been the one between her legs. Now William could usurp the place her master had once held.

William unfastened his trousers and she felt the swollen head of his cock against her sex. She raised her head to watch his face as he slid himself inside her, inch by slow, powerful inch, until he was buried deep inside her. Here was a different kind of spark, a different charge to awaken her true potential. The electricity they generated between them was wholly their own.

He rocked his hips as he moved in and out, never taking his eyes off hers. They shone with such intensity it was like staring at the sun. Justine clenched herself around his cock and he moaned with pleasure, growing even harder. She locked her legs around him and pulled him deeper, urging him to fuck her harder, rougher. He didn't admonish her for telling him what she wanted and she knew he never would. Instead he obliged by slamming his hips against her wildly, pounding her, and she fell back, clutching the edge of the table with both hands and holding on for dear life. She wanted all he could give her, all his passion, power and pain.

He fucked her hard. Brutally, ruthlessly. She gasped and screamed with every thrust, digging her heels into his back to urge him further. Overcome with desire, she tore open his shirt at the front and her hands burrowed beneath the material to clutch at his broad back, where she raked her fingernails over his skin. He arched back, hissing through his teeth, his eyes gleaming with ecstasy. They were in a world of their own creation, a world where pain became pleasure and nothing was forbidden.

He lowered his face to hers, bruising her mouth with harsh kisses as he continued to fuck her, using her the way no one else could – or would. She gasped for breath as he pulled away and slowed his rhythm, sliding nearly all the way out before driving himself in again. And again. And again.

His fingers trailed over her face, down her throat and over her chambermaid's uniform. He wrenched the pinafore aside and grasped her breasts through the material of her black dress. He squeezed her, kneading the soft flesh until she begged him to strip her. The dress parted with a magnificent rip as he tore his way into it to find her, peeling her out of her chemise and falling on her ripe nipples, kissing, licking and biting. Justine flung her arms out behind her so she could lever herself up, giving him better access.

Her body tingled as the pleasure began to mount, carrying her into almost unbearable bliss. William felt her urgency and began to slide his cock in and out of her with even more vigour. He was timing himself, holding off until they could climax together. His control sent a little thrill through her and she knew it wouldn't take her long.

When she felt the first rising throbs she twined her

fingers in his hair and clutched him even tighter with her legs. She wanted to lose herself in him, melt into him until they were a single being, a magnificent creature not of this world. The spasms tore through them both like lightning, making Justine leap and buck helplessly, while he remained strong and unyielding, emptying himself into her.

She screamed as she came, then collapsed, weak and trembling, beneath him. For several seconds she lay there, her eyes closed and her breathing ragged, feeling as though she could float up and away. William was her gravity. He held her down, anchored her back to the world. *Their* world.

'I love you,' she breathed, her voice barely capable of speech.

Although her eyes were still closed, she knew he was smiling. Euphoria emanated from him like heat waves. He kissed her and then whispered in her ear, 'I love *you*. I've always loved you.'

She blinked, opening her eyes. 'Always?'

'I was here the night you were born,' he said. 'Or rather – reborn.' He looked up and she followed his gaze to the skylight. 'I saw you unwrapped, like a butterfly from a cocoon, and I knew you were meant for me. But it wasn't until that night by the river that I saw you truly spread your wings.'

The image of his face blurred as tears filled her eyes

and she clung to him. 'My guardian angel,' she murmured. Then she mustered a cheeky grin for him. 'Or is it devil?'

It was several minutes before she had the strength to get up. Her dress was ruined. Again. 'You're always destroying my clothes,' she said, then giggled.

He stroked her face. 'I prefer to think I'm releasing you from them.'

She couldn't be anything but pleased by the symbolism. It was a shame Frankenstein wouldn't get to see the tatters of her uniform.

'Come on,' said William, adjusting his own clothing. 'We'd better go before he comes back.'

Justine wrapped the remnants of her dress about her like a cloak, hopped down from the table and turned towards the door. Then she froze. Frankenstein was standing there. In his hand he held a pistol, aimed at William.

CHAPTER FIFTEEN

The Bride

'You!'

Frankenstein's face was a mask of horror as he stared in open-mouthed shock at William. The gun wavered for a moment but then he caught himself and raised it back up.

'You,' he said again, the word clearly the culmination of all his worst fears. 'I never thought I would see you again.'

'Nor I you,' William stated coldly.

'But you were dead.'

'Oh, come now, Doctor. You of all people should know that death needn't be the end. You were so confident you were rid of me you never even noticed what was right before your eyes. I've been sitting in on your lectures, watching and learning. Did you never sense me there? Never feel the presence of a monster? Yes, that's how you referred to me in your journal. Naturally, I learned quite a lot from that too. You were very meticulous in your notes on – what was your other name for me? Ah, yes. "Experimental Subject A."'

Frankenstein's eyes blazed with contempt as it all sank in. Justine imagined he was scouring the faces of his student audience in his memory, searching for the one he should have recognised, the one with the prominent duelling scar and the steely, fascinated gaze. The one he should have spotted. The one who would some day be his undoing.

William gestured dismissively at the weapon. 'Would you destroy your "creation"? Take back the life you gave me? And Justine as well?'

'I didn't make her for *you*.'

'You didn't *make* her at all.'

Frankenstein gave a harsh bark of laughter at that. 'Didn't I? This shameless harlot you see before you was as chaste as a nun before I stepped in. Now look at her. The thoughts running ceaselessly through that pretty head would scandalise the most depraved of brothels.'

He indicated her with the pistol and Justine saw William's eyes flash, both at the insult and at the too-small window of opportunity. The gun had only moved away for a second; now it was pointing at William again.

'Don't be a fool,' William said, keeping his voice calm and reasonable. 'Someone will hear the shots. You'll go to prison. Your reputation, your future, your entire life will be ruined.'

'And if I let you go,' Frankenstein said with a sardonic smile, 'I suppose you'll abandon her and leave me in peace?'

'No. She's coming with me.'

Frankenstein shook his head. 'That's not going to happen.'

Justine swallowed her fury and her pride and took a step forward, intending to pacify her erstwhile master. Her dress hung in ragged strips about her shoulders, leaving most of her body exposed. Once he might have taken notice, but now he was blinded by hate. And possibly madness. 'Please –'

'That's close enough, my girl,' Frankenstein growled, keeping the gun pointed at William.

'Listen,' she continued, staying where she was. 'We'll leave you in peace. We'll disappear and you'll never hear from either of us again.'

'You don't seem to understand,' Frankenstein said, his voice almost cheerful now that he had control of the situation. 'You –' he indicated William '– are going back where you came from while you ...' He shook his head sadly at Justine. 'I'm afraid you still need quite a lot of work. And now that there's no need to hide the truth from you any longer I can simply get on with what I need to do.'

'And what is that?' she asked, lifting her chin.

'Correcting the mistakes I made the first time. I'll have to take you to pieces and completely rebuild you. There is no alternative. You don't seem to feel pain in any meaningful sense of the word, so it shouldn't be too uncomfortable for you. Who knows? You may even enjoy it. In any event, when I'm finished you'll be as meek and subservient as you were before. Only this time your submission will be genuine. As will your gratitude towards your master.'

'You're right that she doesn't feel pain,' William said coolly as he advanced, 'but neither do I.'

He lunged for the pistol but Frankenstein got off a shot before William could grab it. The bullet missed and hit the tank, which exploded in a spray of water and glass. Justine covered her face as shards of ice and broken glass rained down on her. She was drenched in icewater and bleeding in several places. And while it didn't hurt, she was alarmed by the sight of her own blood. The blood made everything horribly real.

There was another shot followed by a terrible crash as the table overturned. Glass bottles smashed on the stone floor and a struggle ensued. She opened her eyes to see the two men grappling at each other's throat. They turned in a circle as though they were dancing.

The gun lay nearby on the floor. Both men spied it at the same time but Justine got to it first. With quaking arms she raised the pistol and pointed it at Frankenstein. He stared at her in disbelief.

'You wouldn't dare,' he said, but she heard the uncertainty in his voice.

'I don't want to,' she told him, 'but I will if I have to.'

Frankenstein glared at them both, breathing hard from the scuffle. His icy calm had vanished and Justine watched the play of emotions across his features. She knew exactly what he was thinking and feeling and he had run out of options. Mad he might be, but he was certainly no fool.

After a moment his shoulders sagged in resignation. 'Very well,' he said. 'Have it your way. You were both flawed as it is. I'm sure I can do better.'

'I'm sure you can too,' William said, unperturbed, 'but it won't be here.'

'What do you mean?'

'You're going away, Frankenstein. Into exile. I'm sure you can find some isolated castle in Switzerland or the Carpathian Mountains and resume your so-called "work" there. It's not for us to judge you. After all –' he slipped an arm around Justine '– you did give us life. Again.'

'And each other,' Justine said, pressing close to William.

'Well, isn't this a pretty little love story,' Frankenstein said with venom. He crossed his arms over his chest. 'And supposing I don't indulge this fancy of yours? What then?'

William took the pistol from Justine and cocked it. 'Then I'd have to shoot you.'

'A very happy ending that would be,' Frankenstein scoffed. 'You rotting in prison for murder while she visits you and weeps over your foolishness.'

'Oh no. You forget I have your journals. I know as much as you do about reanimation. And I thank you for that education. But I might just have to put it to use and I don't think you'd enjoy your new life in our service.'

Frankenstein's eyes flashed at the indignity of the suggestion and he opened his mouth to retort. William cut him off.

'Of course, there is another option. I could just shoot you in the leg and incapacitate you. You know what a prolonged and painful healing process that would involve. And if that wasn't enough to bring you to your senses, I would always have the option of publishing your work. I'm sure you'll agree it's not really fit for public consumption so I can only imagine what the authorities would make of your experiments, to say nothing of your less than ethical private practice.'

'Who would believe it? I can't see you two offering yourselves as proof to denounce me.'

'Yes, you're probably right. They would dismiss your journals as merely the ravings of a madman. And I'm sure they'd want to see that the poor deluded wretch who wrote them got the very best care the madhouse could provide. You certainly wouldn't want for company. I hear they let the public in to stare at the lunatics for a penny. Your dear friend Dr Pretorius might even come to see you, to mourn the loss to medical science.'

Frankenstein listened in silence. There was no point in trying to fight the inevitable; he knew he was beaten. Every avenue of escape had been blocked. He dropped his arms to his sides and stared at his feet, looking deflated. 'Very well. What happens now?'

'What happens now is that the kind and generous Dr Frankenstein is delighted by the news that his maid Justine, of whom he was always very fond, is to wed one of his most promising medical students.'

Justine's heart swelled and she watched William admiringly as he spoke. He had thought of everything.

'And, as a wedding present, he leaves this house and all its contents to the happy couple before going abroad. His friend Dr Pretorius goes with him. Together they're sure they can make their fortune in some other country. Neither one of them ever returns to London. That's how this story ends.'

Frankenstein heaved a weary sigh, but he was clearly out of ideas. 'You win.' Then he added with a shrug, 'I was tired of this place anyway.'

'Good. Then I suggest you go and talk to Pretorius. You have some travel arrangements to make. I'm sure he'll be more than happy to accompany you. After all, he must know how dangerous it might be for him too if Scotland Yard were to come sniffing around. They might find his tiny lady-friend and I expect he would have rather a difficult time trying to explain how she came about.'

Scowling, Frankenstein turned to go.

'Oh, and, Frankenstein, I advise you not to try anything foolish. Remember Daisy? She knows the whole story. She's keeping your original journal safe for me and if anything were to happen to either of us ... Well, you're a clever man. I'm sure you can imagine the rest.'

Frankenstein slammed the door behind him.

Justine shook her head in bewilderment. 'You know Daisy?'

'I do now. I paid her a visit on my way here, to give her the journal for safekeeping.'

'Do you really think he'll leave us alone?'

William nodded confidently. 'As I said, he's a clever man. He can make a fresh start somewhere else. The last thing he wants is the risk of being caged up in prison or an asylum for the rest of his life. Whatever it costs him is a small price to pay.'

'You're a genius,' she murmured, kissing him.

'And you're in a bit of a state, my love. Let's get those injuries seen to and then we'll see about finding you some clothes befitting a bride.'

Justine closed her eyes with pleasure and held still as William set about carefully bandaging her wounds. None of the cuts was serious, but she didn't ask him to stop. She stood before him, naked and passive, as he lovingly tended each little cut and scratch. There was a line of small nicks along her right arm and William wound a roll of gauze around her wrist and continued until the entire arm was bound. Then, smiling, he did the same with her other arm. Then her legs. And then, just for good measure, the rest of her body.

She sighed and twisted in his grasp as he ran a length of gauze up between her legs, pulling it tight against her sex and anchoring it over first one shoulder, then the other. The pressure was exquisite and she whimpered softly, both a plea and a protest. His eyes glinted and he shook his head.

'There will be plenty of time for that later, my darling,' he chided her. 'We have the rest of our lives. I want to show you the world, take you to all the places I've been, teach you everything I know.'

'Do you really know more than Frankenstein?'

'So much more,' he said cryptically. 'I know all the secrets that eluded him.'

'Will you show me?'

'You'll see for yourself. In time. We have eternity.'

He wound several bandages around her breasts, pressing them tightly against her chest. Her nipples stood out in sharp relief. He tied off the last of the gauze and smiled, admiring his handiwork. 'You look like an Egyptian queen, placed in her jewelled sarcophagus hundreds of years ago and waiting to be reawakened from her long slumber.'

'I've always dreamt of seeing the great pyramids.'

'You'll see them,' he promised. 'You'll see everything. I'm looking forward to unwrapping you.'

The constricting bandages were a sweet torment. They both suppressed and intensified her sense of touch. Justine knew that, when he released her, her skin would be tingling and highly stimulated from its bondage. She would be desperate for release, craving his touch.

'Am I to be reborn again?' she asked dreamily.

'Yes. This time as *my* creation.' He pressed his lips to hers and squeezed her bandaged breasts, making her shudder. He slid his hand up the inside of one bound thigh and rested his palm against the pulsing warmth he found at its apex.

Justine closed her eyes and curled into his arms. She could hardly wait to begin their new life together. But first she had one request to make. She was sure he would grant it.

EPILOGUE

130 years later

The lights of London twinkle like a scattering of gemstones across the velvet night as Justine opens the curtains. As much as she loves all the great and wonderful cities of the world, there is no place she would rather be than London. This is where she was born. Twice. This is the place she will always call home. It is where she belongs.

Outside a storm is brewing. Soon rain will spatter the windows and a brisk wind will whip the trees in the park below into a frenzy. The heavens mutter with thunder and lightning claws at the sky as the storm edges closer and closer, as though the dark weather is stalking her. But the ominous rumblings only make her smile.

As she stands gazing out at the night she can't help but feel a twinge of nostalgia for the old days. The city has grown more glitzy and glamorous with time, but there is something inescapably romantic about the days of gaslight and fog. She misses the clip-clop of horses' hooves and the rattle of carriage wheels on cobbled streets, the cries of newspaper boys touting the headlines, the call of the flower girls in Covent Garden. But, while the city has undergone dramatic transformations over the years, Justine has not aged a day.

She gives a wistful little sigh and a pair of arms encircles her. The fingers deftly seek out the buttons of her long silk dress and unfasten them slowly, one by one. Justine is wearing nothing underneath. The dress slips to the floor with a whisper and she stands naked before the London night as the hands cup her bare breasts, cool fingers tweaking and teasing her nipples into stiff little knots. Soft lips kiss a trail down her spine, making her skin prickle with sweet anticipation.

All at once the sky opens and the rain begins to fall. It splashes like ocean waves against the windows as lightning flares in the sky. But instead of thunder Justine hears a low insistent humming. For a moment she is puzzled and then she smiles. Fingertips gently tap against her inner thighs, urging her legs apart. She takes a tiny step out to each side, opening herself. Then she rises on tiptoe and gasps as she feels the vibrator pressed firmly up between her legs.

With a whimper of pleasure Justine stretches out her arms, placing her palms against the rain-streaked window. She closes her eyes as the tiny device works its magic and she struggles to stay on her feet. At first it is manageable, a steady flutter she is able to cope with. But then it shifts into a higher gear and the resultant powerful buzzing feels like the engine of a sports car. She writhes and twists in response to the stimulation, losing herself in the inescapable vibrations. Sometimes it only takes a few seconds but tonight she is delighted that it lasts longer.

She imagines someone far out there in the night, watching her lewd performance through a telescope as she squirms and gasps. A naked woman making a shameless exhibition of herself for anyone at all to see. Once upon a time such behaviour would have been called 'moral insanity'. The thought both delights and amuses her. She would have worn the label like a badge of honour.

When the climax comes she arches her body and leans forwards into the window, pressing her breasts against the glass as she cries out, squeezing her thighs around the device. Her legs tremble as wave after wave of delirious pleasure surges through her and finally she sinks to her knees, panting and gasping.

'Welcome home. Did you miss me?'

Justine smiles. 'You know we always miss you, Daisy.'

She turns to look up at her friend. Daisy offers her a radiant smile, still as young and beautiful as the day of their very first kiss. The day she came to the door of Frankenstein's house with a handful of flowers to lay at her friend's grave.

'How was the Valley of the Kings?' Daisy asks.

'Oh, you know,' Justine says, getting to her feet. 'Crazy. Overrun with tourists. Nowhere near as exotic or unspoilt as when the three of us went there last century. I can still remember how magical it all was back then.'

Daisy nods. 'Those were the days, eh? Still, the march of time isn't all bad.' She holds up the vibrator with a wink.

'Hey, I'm not complaining. Technology is a good thing. Jeez, remember that enormous steam-powered machine?' She laughs. 'I dream of seeing one of those on display at the British Museum some day.'

'Or for sale in fetish shops.'

'It did the business, though.'

Daisy laughs. 'It certainly did!'

'Are you ladies actually pining for a rickety old Victorian contraption when you've got a perfectly good man right here?'

Justine smiles as William closes the front door and Daisy leaps into his arms, kissing him hello. He is the only man she trusts with her sexual affections. The years are strewn with women she has loved and left behind, but Justine is and has always been her only true love.

'What took you so long?' Justine asks. 'I thought you were just parking the car.'

William shakes water from his hair and triumphantly holds aloft a bottle. 'Champagne. How can we celebrate coming home without it?'

Daisy tuts. 'I'd have gone out for it,' she says. 'Sometimes I miss my days of playing lady's maid and valet to Sir and Madame.'

'In that case,' William says, handing her the bottle, 'you can do the honours.'

With a cheeky grin Daisy drops a curtsey and disappears into the kitchen.

Justine picks up her dress and considers putting it back on, but William shakes his head. Smiling, she lets the flimsy garment fall to the floor again and returns to the window. The glass streams with water, blurring the lights of the city.

'You made it back just in time,' she says. 'There's a monster of a storm coming.'

'Nature at her worst. Or in our case – best. We wouldn't be here without the lightning.'

'Hey, we're here because of *you*,' she purrs, pressing her naked body up against him. 'I'll never stop reminding you of that. Or thanking you for it.'

From the kitchen comes a loud pop and then the clink of glasses. Moments later Daisy returns, carrying a silver tray with three crystal champagne flutes balanced on it. She is naked but for a frilly white apron tied around her waist. It barely falls low enough to cover her sex and Justine can see that Daisy hasn't shaved while she's been on her own. She will enjoy watching William tidy her up later. It is a ritual that both girls delight in.

'Very nice,' William says approvingly as he takes two of the glasses and hands one to Justine.

Daisy blushes. 'Thank you, sir.' She sets the tray down and lifts her own glass.

'One of us is overdressed,' Justine observes with a sly grin.

'All in good time, ladies,' William says. 'First – a toast. To the two loveliest creatures of this – or any – century.'

'Make that three,' Justine says, and their glasses kiss brightly.

Lightning blooms in the sky outside, accompanied by a ferocious thunderclap that rattles the windowpanes.

Daisy gives a startled little cry and then relaxes into a nervous laugh. 'How very dramatic!' she exclaims.

The night strobes with lightning again, momentarily bathing them in a flash of light. Thunder roars like a beast awakened from a long slumber. The light fittings flicker several times and then wink out, plunging the room into darkness. They stand for a moment in shadow, listening. The rain has turned to hail as the storm's fury escalates.

William's silhouette detaches from the group. 'I'll get some candles.'

Justine smiles, remembering many nights illuminated only by candles or gaslight. Daisy presses her friend's hand in the dark and squeezes it as though reading her thoughts. They have always loved such storms.

Soon William returns, bearing a candelabrum before

him like a torch. The contours of his face dance in the glow of the tiny flames. 'Come, my dears,' he says, beckoning theatrically.

Justine takes his hand and follows him into the bedroom, drawing Daisy behind her.

The luxurious room resembles a seraglio. It is draped in rich velvet curtains and strewn with ornate carpets. An oversized four-poster bed stands on one side of the room and Justine can see that Daisy has made it up with her favourite decadent red satin sheets. Justine dives into the cool softness of the bed while William sets the candelabrum down on a table. Shadows leap and dance along the walls. She thinks there is nothing quite like being warm and safe inside while a tempest rages outside.

'Draw the curtains, Daisy,' Justine urges. 'I want to see the storm.'

'Champagne and candlelight are never enough for our Justine,' William says indulgently.

Daisy tucks the heavy curtains to each side of the two large picture windows, securing them with gold braided cords. The city lies beyond, pelted with rain and sparkling with all the colours of the night.

As they watch, several patches of light blink out as buildings throughout the city lose power. It's as though the three of them are feeding off the city's electricity. A frightening thought, but one Justine finds strangely arousing.

'It's a perfect night for mystery and horror,' she says dreamily. 'The air itself is filled with monsters.'

Light leaps in the sky and Daisy moves away from the window with a start. 'It always makes me nervous,' she says with an embarrassed little laugh.

'We'll protect you,' William tells her, stroking her exposed bottom below the bow of her apron.

'Mmm, thank you, sir,' Daisy murmurs. Then she turns and helps him out of his coat and jacket, making a show of dusting them down with her hand as she lays them across the plush divan at the foot of the bed.

'Such a good little maid,' he says, holding out his arms so Daisy can unbutton his cuffs. 'Don't you think so, my dear?'

'A very good little maid,' Justine agrees. She finishes her glass of champagne and sets it down on the marble-topped nightstand.

Daisy squirms in delight at the praise and sinks to her knees before William to remove his shoes and socks. She tidies them away, taking her time before returning to help him with his trousers. Justine eyes the bulge of his erection hungrily. The last lingering throbs of her orgasm have faded and already she is hungry for more. But this time she wants both of them, together.

Naked at last, William grasps one end of the bow on Daisy's apron but Justine stops him.

'No, leave it on,' she says.

Daisy's cheeks flush with excitement and she lowers her head submissively, pressing her legs together.

William places a hand on top of Daisy's head and gently guides her down onto her knees again. Now it is Justine's turn to squirm as she watches the little maid stroke her husband's cock. The round peach of her bottom is visible below the white strings of her apron, an adorable sight. Daisy slides her hand down over the shaft, squeezing it tightly at the base. Then she plants loving little kisses up and down its length before drawing her tongue along the same path. William sighs with pleasure and grips the nearest bedpost to steady himself against the onslaught of her eager mouth.

Daisy teases him for a while and then she parts her lips and takes him in, filling her mouth and throat with him. Justine slips silently from the bed and steals behind him, running her fingernails up and down his back while Daisy sucks him off. Justine kisses him, stroking his lean, muscular chest and enjoying his breathless moans. Under her hands Justine can feel the vibrations of his body as Daisy brings him to the edge.

After a time he stiffens, shudders and grips the bedpost tightly as his knees bend and he comes hard, his buttocks clenching with each spasm. Daisy holds him tightly and dutifully swallows every drop. Then she grins up at both of them like a happy pet. Justine fetches one of their champagne glasses and holds it to

Daisy's lips. She drinks gratefully, her eyes sparkling with submissive pleasure.

'*Very* good girl,' William says appreciatively, a little out of breath.

Daisy beams with pride. She's had more years than anyone alive to perfect her talents. They all have. And they each know one another intimately, beyond mere flesh and blood.

'I really missed you,' Daisy says. 'Both of you.'

Justine strokes her face. 'You could have come with us, you know.'

'I know. But I like the hunt too. Believe me, I didn't sit here pining while you were gone. I made a few new friends.' She blushes as though the admission actually embarrasses her.

But Justine and William know better. It's all part of the game for Daisy. She seduces lovely young girls into believing they've seduced *her*, then revels in the idea that she's been coaxed into something she wouldn't otherwise have done. It's been her *modus operandi* since William and Justine first took her up to the laboratory and told her the whole fantastic story. She hadn't needed any real convincing to join them, just the illusion thereof.

Daisy bats her eyes and looks down at the floor, an invitation neither of them can resist. Justine pushes her down onto the bed and sits astride her before lowering her head to kiss her. Daisy opens her mouth eagerly and

Justine pushes her tongue inside, swirling it around as she runs her nails up and down Daisy's warm body. She tastes of champagne and spices.

She cups Daisy's breasts in her hands and pushes her face into their pillowy softness, kissing and licking her, revelling in the lovely difference between male and female bodies.

Soon she feels William's hand on her shoulders as he urges her gently forward. She relaxes her weight against Daisy, their breasts pressed together. Suddenly Daisy gives a little squeak and then Justine reacts as William slides a finger inside her as well. He fucks them with his hands while they kiss and caress each other, grinding their hips, pelvis to pelvis, breasts to breasts.

It takes no time at all before Daisy trembles and clutches at Justine, crying out as a powerful climax races through her. Her hips quiver and she forces her mound hard up against Justine's, letting her feel the little pulses that make her sigh with satisfaction. Daisy doesn't bask in her own afterglow for long, however. She is always more eager to please others.

With a coy smile, Daisy slips out from underneath Justine and pushes her down on her back. Then she moves down to her legs and gently eases them apart.

Justine closes her eyes as William gathers her small breasts in his hands and then she feels his lips close around first one nipple, then the other. Her breathing grows deeper and heavier as his tongue begins to swirl round each hard little bud in lazy circles.

Daisy presses her lips to the hollow of Justine's inner thigh and draws her fingers up along the slick crease of her sex with agonising deliberation. Justine gives a petulant little moan and she thrusts her hips up, begging, demanding. At last she feels Daisy's tongue. It flutters against Justine's delicate clit, making her jump and gasp.

She clutches the headboard as sensations are heaped on her by both lovers. Lips, tongues and hands blur into a haze of pure pleasure and she abandons herself to their ministrations. Whenever her thighs start to clench, Daisy guides them firmly apart again with surprisingly strong hands. Now her face is buried between Justine's legs, her tongue flicking back and forth across the most sensitive part of her, never pausing for a moment in its relentless, delicious caress.

They are all intimately familiar with the needs of one another's bodies and Justine is lost entirely to the joy of total indulgence. Occasionally she struggles only to be reminded that two are more powerful than one. William crosses her wrists together and holds them pinned with one hand while he stimulates her body with the other. His fingers seek out every sensitive place, stroking, kneading and teasing her, while Daisy continues to kiss her sex, rapidly bringing her to the very peak of ecstasy and then easing off again.

Justine whimpers each time, thinking she is about to come, only to be denied. She has no doubt they are exchanging wicked glances as they tease and torment her, delighting in her helplessness and desperation.

By the time William and Daisy allow her to come she is in a frenzy of need, her body hyper-stimulated by Daisy's earlier ambush. The climax hits her with devastating force, wrenching a scream from her like the cry of some wild animal. Her body succumbs to wave after wave of throbbing pleasure and she feels it in every bone, every muscle, every inch of flesh.

She lies for a long time with her eyes closed, panting and basking in the bliss of release. After a while a glass is pressed to her lips and she drinks the proffered champagne greedily, purring with satisfaction.

But it is only the beginning. The night is still young. The three lovers pass the hours in playful debauchery and, when they are at last exhausted, they collapse in a tangle of arms and legs. Outside the storm continues, unabated. Lightning flashes in the sky above while down below three of its creatures sleep and dream of forever.